The voice in his head

Joey pressed his hands over his ears. Nothing. So far he had heard the voice only at night, every night since Friday, drilling the same words into his brain:

The door in the lake, the door in the lake—come.

When he finally managed to fall asleep, the words invaded his dreams. But by morning the voice was gone. All that remained was a whooshing sound, like air blowing from an electric fan or the rush of a distant stream. A faint, high-pitched hum whined in the background, as if a gnat were buzzing in his ear.

Was this what it was like to go crazy—hearing a voice that wasn't your own inside your head?

"The suspense builds to a surprising climax that leaves you wondering: If time can stop, can it also go backward?"
—*Booklist*

"Butts grounds the paranormal action in everyday life, and wraps up the story in a water-tight climax. An agreeable diversion for UFO enthusiasts." —*Publishers Weekly*

The Door
in the Lake

Nancy Butts

SCHOLASTIC INC.

New York Toronto London Auckland Sydney
Mexico City New Delhi Hong Kong

For my parents,
Thomas and Elizabeth Cobbledick,
who always believed in me

ISBN 0-439-29788-5

12 11 10 9 8 7 6 5 4 3 2   1 2 3 4 5 6/0

Printed in the U.S.A.   40

First Scholastic printing, April 2001

Penetrating so many secrets, we cease
to believe in the unknowable. But
there it sits, nevertheless,
calmly licking its chops.
—H. L. Mencken

The Door in the Lake

CHAPTER ONE

Monday, October 7, 6:00 A.M.

The glass door swung open and a flurry of dead leaves, red and yellow and brown, skittered across the cracked linoleum floor.

The boy's reflection bulged in the wide-angle mirror over the cash register, head pumped up like one of those shiny Mylar balloons full of helium, arms and legs so shrunken they looked as fragile and stick-like as a spider's.

Mr. Patel kept his eye on the boy as he rang up coffee and a six-pack of pecan twirls for the truck driver.

The trucker, who had the name LEVON stitched over the pocket of his shirt, craned his neck around to follow the storekeeper's gaze.

"I got a boy his age." Levon squinted and rubbed the black stubble on his chin. "About eleven or twelve, I guess. He ain't gonna give you no trouble."

Mr. Patel handed Levon his change and cleared his throat. "Begging your pardon, sir, but I am thinking you don't know much about trouble. My cousin in Mississippi —he has been robbed two times, and by boys not much older than that one."

"I swear," Levon said. "Makes you wonder what in tarnation their folks are up to. Take this one. Not sunup yet, and here he is roaming around by his lonesome. In his bare feet no less."

They both stared at the boy's shoeless feet.

"I catch my boy out of the house this time of night, I'd wear him out good."

Mr. Patel's forehead puckered in confusion. "Wear him out?"

"He'd get a whipping. Better that than out where some pervert could get to him."

The two men studied the boy. Gray sweatpants sagged around his hips. He wore an oversized black T-shirt with a glow-in-the-dark picture of the Milky Way on both sides, the words YOU ARE HERE and an arrow pointing to a tiny white dot near the edge of the spiral. Flakes of skin were beginning to peel off his sun-baked nose. His hair hadn't been washed in days. It was so lank and dirty it could have been any color from chestnut to dark blond.

The boy wandered down the aisles of the convenience store, sniffling and wiping his nose with one hand. He rotated his head mechanically from side to side, as if he were searching the shelves for a can of soup or that box of crackers a mother might have sent him for. But his eyes were blank, twin blue mirrors that reflected everything yet saw nothing.

"There's something funny about him," Levon said, his styrofoam cup of coffee cooling, forgotten, in his hand.

Mr. Patel nodded.

The boy ratcheted his head over one shoulder, like a

robot, and blinked once, his lids jerking open and shut as if there were some kind of electrical short circuit in the nerves to his eyes.

"I am thinking he is on drugs," Mr. Patel whispered. He slid a quarter out of the cash register and edged toward the pay phone on the wall.

The boy hobbled toward the glass-fronted refrigerator case in the back of the store where milk cartons and juice bottles and soft drink cans were lined up in slanted trays like the audience at a theater.

He walked as if he had to think about it first, lifting each leg through the air in slow motion. Gravity always seemed to get the better of him at the last moment and his feet flopped down to the floor.

The boy stopped in front of the dairy case and reached for the handle, staring at his arm as if he had never seen it before.

Mr. Patel slammed the quarter on the counter and marched down the aisle toward the boy, waving his arms in the air. "No, no," he yelled.

The boy turned to face him. Mr. Patel froze at the sight of his glassy, vacant eyes.

"You go, you go now."

The boy ran his tongue across his lips and looked away as if he hadn't heard him or was too thirsty to care. He took a quart of milk off the shelf and fumbled with the spout. Mr. Patel tried to grab it away from him, but the boy clung to it tenaciously. He managed to tear a hole in the top, but before he could drink his glance fell on the back of the carton. Lower lip trembling, he collapsed in a heap, like a puppet whose strings have been cut.

The waxed carton hit the linoleum and burst open, flooding the floor with milk.

Levon ran back and squatted beside the boy. "Musta hit his head—he's out like a light. I'll call the ambulance."

Mr. Patel righted the carton, starting to clean up the spill. He stared back and forth between the container in his hand and the boy who lay unconscious in the spreading pool of milk.

A child grinned from a grainy black-and-white photograph under the logo of a smiling cow.

NAME: Joseph Patrick Finney
HOMETOWN: Cornish Gap, VA
MISSING: Since July 6, two years ago
AGE: 12 years at time of disappearance.
Now 14.
HEIGHT: 4'10"
WEIGHT: 80 lbs.
EYES: Blue
HAIR: Dark brown/straight
TYPE: Presumed stranger abduction
DETAILS: Disappeared while camping
with family in Jefferson National For-
est in Blue Ridge Mountains of south-
western Virginia. Last seen wearing
gray sweatpants and black T-shirt.

"This is the lost boy," Mr. Patel said.

"Hold on a minute," Levon barked into the wall phone, then covered the receiver with one hand. "What did you say?"

"It is the boy on the milk carton. The boy who was kidnapped."

"Get the sheriff over here too," Levon said, and hung up.

The trucker came back and clamped a beefy hand on the boy's shoulder with a tenderness that belied his size.

"I am remembering now," Mr. Patel said. "It was in all the newspapers. They sent reporters from Roanoke and television cameras from as far away as Richmond."

"How long ago was that?"

Mr. Patel consulted the milk carton. "A little more than two years." He frowned.

"Lemme see that," Levon said, grabbing the empty container. His lips moved silently as he read the notice for himself. "Lookie here," he said at last. "You mighta made a mistake. This can't be right."

"No, no, I am certain." Mr. Patel folded his arms across his chest. "I am living in Cornish Gap for eleven years now. Nothing so bad as this ever happened here before."

"Well, according to this, the Finney boy should be fourteen now," Levon persisted. "Does this kid look that old to you?"

Mr. Patel made a clucking noise deep in his throat and backed away.

Sirens wailed in the distance.

Levon scraped his hand over his unshaven face and shook his head.

"I'm telling you," he said, "this can't be the same kid. He don't look no older than the boy in the picture. Don't you get it? He oughta look different."

14

CHAPTER TWO

Wednesday, October 9, 5:00 P.M.

Joey, he remembered. His name was Joey.

Waking up felt like swimming to the surface of an underground river, the air above as black and airless as the water below. He had been drifting in the darkness for a long time before he realized who he was.

He heard noises and knew he was awake, although he still couldn't see or feel anything. But the sounds were all wrong. The squeak of rubber soles on linoleum where he expected chipmunks scrambling for their breakfast outside the tent. The rattle of trays in a metal cart instead of Magnum's dog tags as the Newfoundland shifted at the foot of Joey's sleeping bag. The rush of air from a heater instead of wind through the branches of the pine and hickory trees. So this was what his father meant when he talked about sleeping like a log. It must be the lake air. He had been dead to the world all night.

Joey tried to roll over. Something tugged on his left arm, holding him back like a rein or a leash, and there was a sharp, stinging sensation in his hand. His cheek rubbed up against a smooth surface that smelled faintly of bleach.

A bed. This was wrong too. He should be feeling the

bumps and dips of hard ground under his body, maybe even a few rocks digging into his hip—not a pillow and a mattress.

What was going on here? He had gone to sleep last night at a campground near Smokewater Lake in the national forest. His dog Magnum, his best friend Hamp, his bratty little brother Kevin, and Kevin's friend Travis had all been in the tent beside him. Where were they now? Where was *he?*

Joey tried to open his eyes, but it felt as though they were glued shut. "Mom! Dad?" He did his best to yell, but all that came out was a croak that sounded as if he had swallowed a throatful of gravel.

Fear flooded Joey's body. He catapulted off the pillow, thrashing sideways in the bed and kicking at the sheets. He yanked at the thing that restrained his left arm, ignoring the pain that jabbed into his hand like wasp stings.

"Whoa there," said a strange voice close to his ear. "You're going to pull out your IV."

Joey stopped struggling. He smelled Old Spice, the kind of aftershave he and Kevin gave their dad every year for Father's Day. But this was not his father's voice. Who was it?

"That's the first sign of life you've shown in two days." A hand clamped over his wrist and guided it down to the bed. "Let's try not to damage the merchandise, okay?"

Joey sniffed.

"It's all right to open your eyes."

"I tried," Joey whispered. His tongue and the insides of

his cheeks felt as if they were furred with cotton. "I can't."

The man chuckled and patted Joey's wrist. "I'm sure it feels like you've got lead weights in your eyelids, but give it your best shot. You're just worn out."

Joey willed his eyes to open. Each lid felt as heavy as a garage door, but with a herculean effort he managed to raise them far enough to peer out through narrow slits.

He was in a hospital room. Fluorescent lights buzzed overhead, casting a harsh glow that made the skin of his arms look yellowish green. Through the slats of venetian blinds at the window he could see the round shoulders of the Allegheny Mountains hunched against the sky. Silver rails fenced in his bed like a crib.

He turned to look at a man with tight blond curls and wire-rimmed glasses who stood beside the bed.

The man flashed a penlight in Joey's eyes and nodded. "Looks like most of the cobwebs are gone," he said. "I'm Dr. Kaminsky."

The doctor wasn't wearing a white coat, just corduroy slacks and a turtleneck under a rust-colored chamois shirt. The only sign that he was a doctor was the stethoscope draped around his neck.

"Aren't you hot?" Joey asked, eyeing the turtleneck and corduroys.

"Not for this time of year." Dr. Kaminsky raised an eyebrow. "Can you tell me the date, son?"

"I don't know." Joey counted back. "The fifth, I guess."

"The fifth of what?"

"July." Joey said it slowly. That was a funny question.

"Can you tell me your name?"

Joey frowned. Why didn't the doctor know his name? "Like my parents probably told you already, it's Joey. Joey Finney." He pulled up the sheet and stared at his body, checking for stitches or a cast.

"What happened to me?" A whine crept into his voice. "I mean, the last thing I remember is having to go to the bathroom real bad."

Dr. Kaminsky remained silent. The look on his face made Joey uneasy.

Fluid dripped in Joey's nose. It was an odd feeling, unpleasant, not like a nosebleed but more like something leaking from inside his head that shouldn't be. He turned his head to one side and wiped his nose on his shoulder.

Dr. Kaminsky reached back to the bedside table, picked up a box of tissues, and set it by Joey's free right hand. "We're going to do some more tests to see if we can find out what's causing that," he said.

Joey blew his nose. "What happened to me?" His throat shut so tight it hurt.

"We'll find out, Joey. I promise." Dr. Kaminsky squeezed his wrist. "But right now there are some people who've been waiting to meet you."

The doctor went to the door and stuck his head outside. Joey heard a murmur of voices in the hallway, then Dr. Kaminsky reappeared. He swung the door aside and smiled.

Joey had a moment to wonder why the doctor was smiling at him that way—the way his piano teacher did before a recital, as if to say, "It's all right, you'll live through it"—when his parents walked into the room.

His mother spread her arms wide and rushed to the bed, crushing him in her arms and burying her face in the pillow beside his head. He could feel tears on his neck.

How could her hair turn gray overnight? How could she get so thin and tired since just yesterday?

"Look at him," Joey's father said. Two deep grooves were carved in his face, dragging down the corners of his mouth. "Did this happen from being starved or abused?"

Joey longed for a mirror to see what was wrong with him to make his father act this way.

"He was dehydrated when he was brought in, suffering from exhaustion, and it did appear that he hadn't eaten in several days." Dr. Kaminsky measured his words carefully. "But I found no signs of long-term malnutrition, or for that matter any kind of abuse. As far as I can tell, there isn't any physical cause for the delay in his growth."

"Then how do you explain it?" his father asked. "He doesn't look a day older than when he disappeared."

Disappeared? The word exploded inside Joey like a bomb. What was his father talking about?

"Dad, we played Frisbee together just last night, remember? Up at the lake."

His father's face caved in. "Last night?"

Joey's eyes darted back and forth between the new lines in his father's face and the gray streaks in his mother's hair.

He shot a look at Dr. Kaminsky, then glanced out the

window. He saw a maple tree down in the parking lot, littering the pavement with papery orange leaves. He stared beyond at the mountains and noticed for the first time that they were ablaze with scarlet and gold.

Summer was long gone. How much time had passed since the Fourth of July weekend?

Joey felt as if a giant rubber band were being wrapped around his chest. He struggled to breathe.

"Last night?" his father repeated. "That was two years ago, Joey." He lurched to the side of Joey's bed and clutched him in a bear hug. "Where have you been?"

CHAPTER THREE

Thursday, October 10, 1:00 P.M.

Joey pulled a tissue from a box that was already half empty and wiped his nose. He stared out the car window. The sky hung low, a gray ceiling of clouds that sagged down to touch the mountains.

Mrs. Finney eyed Joey from the front seat. "It looks like your old clothes still fit."

Joey glanced down at the same sweatpants and black T-shirt he'd worn camping. It was a good thing the nurses had washed them for him. He couldn't wear the stuff his mother had brought—a pair of almost-new running shoes, sweatpants, and a sweatshirt. His younger brother Kevin's things, Mom had said. She had tried not to look worried when they didn't fit. Kevin's stuff was way too big for Joey.

He didn't want to think about what that meant.

His father turned the Buick onto Laurel Street.

"Home, Joey," his mother said, her face beaming. "We're almost home."

Joey twisted the shoulder belt between his fingers. The rubbery scrambled eggs he had choked down for breakfast churned in his stomach.

The street was showered with yellow. Yellow ribbons

on mailboxes and porch rails and car antennas. The Stauntons had wrapped a huge yellow bow around the trunk of the sycamore in their front yard, and Mrs. Nuttall had tied dozens of tiny yellow ribbons to the branches of her dogwood. They fluttered in the breeze like a flock of butterflies.

Joey squinted, wincing as if all that color hurt his eyes. "What are the ribbons for?"

"They're for you," his mother said. "Two years is a long time, but nobody in Cornish Gap forgot you." Her voice quavered. "We never gave up hope."

His father slowed the Buick in front of their house. "Where am I supposed to park?"

"Good Lord," his mother whispered. "Patty Staunton said to prepare for a crowd, but I never expected this."

Joey looked out the window. The curb, the sidewalk, even their front lawn, were jammed with cars. People spilled off the front porch into his mother's azaleas. Pointing and waving when they spotted the Buick, they began streaming down to the street.

Joey ducked back, pressing himself into the seat.

His father edged the Buick into the only space available, blocking the end of the driveway, and parked. He switched off the ignition and stepped out just as the swarm of people rushed the car.

"I'll get out first and take your hand, okay?" his mother said. She lifted the handle.

There was a burst of applause and a deafening cheer. Flashbulbs popped and flared. Someone thrust a microphone in their faces. Dazed, Joey shrank back and let his father clear a path to the house.

The house was as crowded as the yard. People swept past him in a dizzying parade—aunts, uncles, his piano teacher, his Scout leader, Father Kinsella from over at St. Jude's, his baseball coach, and every teacher he'd had from kindergarten through the sixth grade. They looked different somehow—their faces puffier, their bodies softer than he remembered.

Everybody he knew was here. Everybody but kids his own age. Where were his friends? Where was Hamp?

One of Joey's aunts grabbed him and marched him to the kitchen. "You must be hungry," she said, pushing a plate of potato salad and ham biscuits at him.

Joey nibbled at a biscuit. "If I could just lie down for a while." He bolted out of the kitchen and fought his way upstairs.

A teenaged boy carrying a small girl pushed past him on the steps, bumping into Joey's chest with his shoulder.

"It's my house," Joey muttered. "You people act like you live here."

"I *do* live here." A deep voice cracked, then zoomed to a higher register.

Joey whirled around.

"Hello, Joey," the teenager said. He didn't smile. Although he was standing one step below Joey, the boy's gray eyes were on a level with his.

"Kevin?" Joey grabbed the banister. He felt as if he was going to fall. His little brother Kevin, exactly one year younger than he. Except he wasn't so little anymore.

Kevin bounced the child lightly on his hip and curled his mouth into a thin smile. "At least I didn't have to give up a perfectly good pair of running shoes—they must have been way too big for you. Put them back in my room, okay?"

Joey looked at the Adam's apple bobbing up and down in Kevin's throat. Joey put his hand to his own throat. It felt smooth and flat.

They stared at each other silently until the toddler Kevin was holding reached up, twined her fingers in his hair, and tugged.

"Appa dooce, Kebin."

"No, no, Molly. Don't pull my hair," he said. "I'll get you some apple juice in a minute." The child plugged her thumb in her mouth and rested her strawberry blond head against Kevin's neck.

This was a new and improved Kevin. Joey had never known his brother to waste any of his precious time with little kids before.

But then he remembered what Mom had told him in the car about his new little sister. "This is Molly?"

Kevin's eyes gleamed. He unwrapped the girl from his side and handed her to Joey.

"Make yourself useful. Get your baby sister some apple juice." Whistling off-key, he skipped down the stairs.

Joey held the child at arm's length. How old was she? She wasn't a baby anymore—her shoes had hard soles for walking. She must be a year at least, probably older.

Joey's arms began to shake. Sister. He really did have a sister.

The child screwed up her face and shrieked.

The room began to spin in nauseating circles around Joey. His father appeared at the bottom of the staircase. His mother rushed up beside him.

"Mommy's here, Molly, it's all right," she crooned in a singsong voice, folding the child in her arms. Then she reached out for Joey and wrapped him in a hug.

Joey pulled away. The shaking spread from his arms to his whole body.

"Oh, Joey." Tears welled up in his mother's eyes.

His father glared at Kevin, who shrugged, his face blank and unreadable as a mask. "I'm ditching this madhouse," Kevin said. "If you want me, I'll be at Travis's." He stalked out the front door.

Joey hurtled down the steps a second later.

"Joey? Kevin? Go after them, Daniel," his mother pleaded. "This is our first time together as a family in over two years."

"Let them go, Beth," his father replied. "This is going to take time for all of us to get used to."

Joey ran to the kitchen and out onto the screened porch. He crouched on the steps, tucking his knees under his chin, and stared at the back yard without seeing it.

Joey's body shook so hard that his muscles began to hurt. What his parents kept saying in the hospital was true. A gigantic chunk of his life had disappeared. He had fallen asleep in a tent at Smokewater Lake and awakened more than two years later in the hospital, with no memory of where he had been or what he had done.

Joey covered his face with his hands.

Something wet and soft prodded his ear. Joey spread his fingers apart and peered through the gaps.

"Magnum!" He reached out to rumple the fur on the dog's massive head.

The dog shook free.

"Not you too! It's me, boy. Don't you remember?"

The Newfoundland began to sniff Joey all over, the way he checked out repairmen and other strangers who came to the house. He spent a long time smelling Joey's nose and hands.

Joey didn't think he could stand it if Magnum started barking at him. He began to rise. He had to get out of there.

But then the dog leaped on his shoulders and forced him back down on the steps, slurping Joey's face with a great warm tongue.

Joey wrapped his arms around Magnum's neck. "See, Mags, I haven't changed. It's everybody else who's different."

He buried his face in the dog's fur. Magnum's familiar smell, earthy but clean, comforted him. Joey clung to him for a long time.

Behind them the screen door to the porch creaked, and Joey felt the wooden steps shake. Magnum barked once, then butted his head underneath the newcomer's arm.

"Bossy devil, aren't you?"

Joey turned. A balding bear of a man, big as a professional football player, loomed behind him. He was wearing a tan shirt with an emblem that read CLOUDLINE COUNTY SHERIFF'S DEPARTMENT on the sleeve.

The man squatted down beside him. "My name is Wade Varnadoe. I'm the sheriff here in Cornish Gap."

Joey slid to the far edge of the step, keeping Magnum between him and the sheriff.

"I'm sorry about that circus out front—afraid we let things get a jump on us. My deputies have got it cleaned out now."

Joey said nothing.

"Your parents said it would be all right if we had a little talk. Is that okay with you?"

Joey rubbed Magnum under the chin and stared down at the ground. "Have I done something wrong?"

"No, son," the sheriff rasped in a deep bass. "Now to your mama and daddy, and most folks hereabouts, your coming home after all this time seems like a happy ending to a long, bad dream."

The sheriff clapped his hand gently between Joey's shoulder blades. Joey jumped.

"But in my seventeen years as a lawman, I've learned that happy endings aren't always what they seem."

Joey shrugged away from the sheriff's hand and scooted off the steps.

"You can talk to me about what happened. That's why I'm here."

Joey wiped his nose with the back of his hand and shook his head. "I don't remember anything."

The flat, white disk of the sun broke through the clouds for a moment, its light glinting off the silver star on the sheriff's shirt pocket. The glare blinded Joey. He shuddered and hid his face in his hands, collapsing to the ground and rolling into a ball.

"Do you smell it?" he asked, sniffing the air.

The sheriff crouched down beside him. "Smell what, son?"

"The light," Joey said. "It's burning."

"Tell me what you see, son," Sheriff Varnadoe said.

Joey's lids fluttered, and his eyes rolled back in their sockets. He remembered.

CHAPTER FOUR

Tuesday, July 5, 1:14 A.M.
Two years earlier

Joey's bladder cramped. He reached over and shook the lump beside him on the floor of the tent. "Hamp. Hamp, wake up," he urged in a harsh whisper. "I gotta go."

There was no response. Some best friend Hamp was. Wouldn't crawl out of his sleeping bag long enough to keep his buddy company on the long, dark hike through the woods to the latrine.

Joey wrinkled his nose. It was dank and stuffy in the tent. The aroma of dog and four unwashed boys mingled with the musty smell of old canvas that had been rained on and packed up wet one time too often.

He heard the jangle of Magnum's collar as the big dog twitched in his sleep, probably chasing a squirrel through his dreams. He jabbed him with one toe. "Get up, boy."

Joey groped for his flashlight and switched it on. The beam glinted off the chrome links in Magnum's choke collar, spotlighting his giant black head.

"Come on, move." Joey slipped one finger through the ring at the end of the dog's collar and tugged hard, but Magnum didn't budge.

"Sleeping Beauty. Don't expect me to kiss you to wake you up."

Joey shook his head. No way he was going to ask his younger brother Kevin or Kevin's dumb friend Travis to go with him. He could hear them now. "What's the matter? Afraid Bigfoot will get you?"

His bladder ached. He would just have to go alone. Joey unzipped his sleeping bag and wriggled free. He fumbled around in the darkness for his sneakers and jammed his feet partway inside, his heels smashing the backs of the shoes flat. He tripped over Hamp in the process, but his friend did not stir.

Joey whistled softly. "You all are really sacked out. It's like night of the living dead in here." His voice sounded loud in the silence.

He hesitated for a minute, then picked his way over four motionless bodies to the tent flap, giving his brother a little kick in the backside as he passed.

Joey crawled through the flap and stood up, the spiral of the Milky Way gleaming a faint green on his T-shirt. The air smelled fresh and piney after the stuffiness of the tent. Although the summer night was warm, Joey shivered a little, a fresh sunburn giving him the chills. He was glad now that Mom had made him pack his sweatpants.

He waved his flashlight across the pup tent where his parents were sleeping, hoping one of them might wake up if he shone the light on them long enough. But neither of them moved. He sighed and swept the flashlight until it illuminated the trailhead to the latrine.

Joey squared his shoulders and began to shuffle down the path. The narrow beam of his flashlight seemed to dim in the pall of darkness that shrouded the trail. A seamless blanket of clouds obscured the moon and stars, making the night even darker.

He should just go here, behind a tree—then he wouldn't have to venture so far away from the campsite—alone in the middle of Jefferson National Forest. Who would see? He'd be back in his sleeping bag in no time, Magnum lying on his feet, Hamp grinding his teeth beside him.

Joey's chest hitched, a sound escaping that was more like a hiccup than a sigh. The rangers said you were supposed to use the latrines. They were built for a reason, to protect this fragile pocket of wilderness. That wouldn't make any difference to Kevin. He'd just go right outside the tent. Hamp too—but not him. Not Joey. He always followed the rules.

He scuffed along the trail as it veered downhill through the trees to skirt the shore of the lake. Joey was struck by the silence. It was absolute. It was never this quiet in the woods. There was always some noise, but not tonight. Tonight he could hear no crickets or frogs or owls, no branches creaking in the wind, no stealthy rustlings of small, unseen forest creatures in the underbrush.

The silence crowded in upon him, so thick he could almost feel it. Something pounded in his ears. It took Joey a while to realize it was the thump of his own heartbeat.

Joey swung his flashlight in a semicircle ahead of him, scanning the darkness for the squat log walls of the latrine. He spotted a sign that read U.S. FOREST SERVICE strung on a cable between two posts, and then the light reflected off a metal latch on the latrine door. Joey hurried in that direction.

He paused, swinging the door back and checking for spiders, chasing shadows away with his flashlight. Then, tucking it under one arm and pinching his nose to keep out the smell, Joey rushed inside.

The moment he was finished he pulled up his sweatpants and hopped outside. What a relief. Now he would run all the way back to his tent. Then he noticed the lake.

Cocking his head to one side, Joey frowned and edged closer to the shore. What was this? The entire lake, all the way across to the far side, glowed milky white, as if a star were sunk beneath the surface. He crouched down at the water's edge and saw the silhouettes of tiny fish streaming back and forth in the radiance.

Joey backed away, then whirled around and started up the path that led to Magnum and his parents and the safety and ordinariness of the campsite. That's when he smelled it. Not the sour, fetid odor he would have expected this close to the latrine, and not the sharp clean scent of pine trees either. This was something different, a burnt smell that curled the hairs inside his nose. It reminded him of electricity in the air before a thunderstorm, or that time the wires from the toaster shorted out and the cord melted.

Don't turn around, Joey told himself, just go back to the tent.

But when he tried to pick up his feet to move, he felt the ground beneath him vibrating, shock waves tingling through the bones of his body all the way to his teeth.

His flashlight began to flicker wildly, turning itself off and then blazing back into life far brighter than its two C batteries should have been able to spark.

Joey had the sudden strange sensation that his skin and scalp were loose, and he clapped his hand on top of his head. His hair was standing straight in the air, all three inches of it. Even the fine hairs along his arms floated upright.

Dirt and pine needles and crumbled leaves swirled around in miniature dust devils on the ground, although there was not a breath of wind. As he watched, the metal cable between the two signposts bowed upward and stretched tight. He heard a steady, low humming sound, and the U.S. FOREST SERVICE sign rotated until it was standing straight up.

He froze, rooted to the spot, until the quaking of the earth beneath his feet spun him around to face the lake. A kaleidoscope of ripples agitated the surface of the water as the unearthly light grew brighter.

Joey felt the tremors rattling through his feet and legs. Between the gnarled roots of an old pine, the ground moved up and down, as if the earth itself were breathing. The ripples on the lake swelled into waves, and he saw several small whirlpools pocking the water. The only sound he could hear was the monotonous hum of the sign cable.

And then an immense circle emerged from the lake.

The spit dried up in Joey's mouth.

The moon was rising out of Smokewater Lake.

But it wasn't the moon. The circle was spinning, tunneling a hole through the sky. A riot of color—electric blues, fluorescent greens, neon reds, acid yellows, and incandescent purples—blazed and whirled in a dervish dance of light.

Joey shaded his eyes with one hand and turned his head away from the glare. The hole gaped above him, wide as the mouth of a hungry giant, and Joey's mind blanked, erased clean by the impossibility of what was happening.

He floated upward.

His flashlight and a pair of dirty sneakers, their backs squashed flat, dropped to the ground.

CHAPTER FIVE

Thursday, October 10, 1:45 P.M.

Blades of grass tickled the corner of his mouth. A pebble dug into his right cheekbone. The smell of damp earth filled his nose and throat.

He wouldn't think about it.

Joey blinked several times and tried to bring the world into focus. The vision on his right side was blocked. He rolled his left eye around and saw a patch of sky criss-crossed with branches, a roofline canted at a crazy angle.

Hot breath blew against the side of his neck. With great effort, Joey turned his head and brought Magnum's black muzzle into view. The dog nudged him with a wet nose.

A knee jutted in his face and Joey heard a voice rumbling. He couldn't make out the words. There was something wrong with his ears. They were filled with noise—crackling static and a muted whine that sounded like the dead air between stations on a radio dial.

Sheriff Varnadoe's face appeared. His mouth moved and Joey strained to hear.

"Tell me what you saw, son," the sheriff was saying.

Nobody would believe him.

• • •

"From what Joey tells me, and what Wade Varnadoe described, I think it's likely that Joey experienced a seizure of some kind," Dr. Kaminsky said.

He perched on the edge of the gurney, fiddling with the bell of the stethoscope draped around his neck. Beyond the curtains that enclosed the table and made a cramped examination space, Joey could hear a baby wailing outside in the emergency room. He hadn't managed to stay out of the hospital for even one full day.

"A seizure?" His mother's fingers twisted in her lap. "Joey's never had a seizure before."

The lines tugging down the corners of his father's mouth sharpened. "Not that we know of. But then we don't know what might have happened during the past twenty-seven months."

Joey stared up at the ceiling. The noise in his ears had died down, but he could still hear a faint hiss, as if the sound were coming from far away.

Dr. Kaminsky shifted his weight. "How are you holding up, sport?" he asked Joey. "Any headache? Your back hurt?"

Joey sniffed and shook his head.

The doctor turned back to Joey's parents. "Calling what happened to Joey a seizure is just giving it a name. A seizure is only a symptom, a description—not a disease in itself. We have to probe deeper to find out what caused the seizure, and if he's likely to have another. I'd like to do another test, a CAT scan. That will give us a detailed picture of the inside of Joey's skull."

"The inside of my skull?" Joey said. "You're not going to stick anything in my head, are you?"

"It's just an x-ray." Dr. Kaminsky patted Joey's arm. "You won't feel a thing."

"What are you looking for?" Joey's father asked.

His mother glanced at Joey and leaned forward in her chair, dropping her voice to a whisper. "Maybe we should talk somewhere else."

"Joey can hear anything I have to say, Mrs. Finney. I don't think it's a brain tumor, if that's what you're worried about. Not given his age and symptoms, though of course the CAT scan will rule that out."

She sagged back in her chair and sighed. "Then what?"

"Well, the EEG was normal," Dr. Kaminsky explained. "The electrodes I pasted to Joey's head monitored his brain waves, and we found nothing wrong there. But then we wouldn't expect to between seizures."

The doctor continued, almost as if he were talking to himself. "The results of the lumbar puncture were more informative."

Joey flinched, remembering the stab of the needle in his back.

"I can't say for sure what might be going on until after this last test. It's an intriguing pattern: amnesia, the persistent runny nose, an apparent seizure." Dr. Kaminsky turned and gazed at Joey with calm blue eyes. "I'm hoping Joey will help me out. We need to talk some more."

Joey licked dry lips. He didn't know which made him more nervous—the CAT scan or the prospect of trying to answer Dr. Kaminsky's questions without lying.

"So, Mr. and Mrs. Finney, with your permission, I'd like to get started."

His mother gathered her cardigan and purse and stood up. She reached over and stroked Joey's face. "We'll see you in a little while, honey."

"It will be fine, Joey," his father said, drawing back the curtain and edging outside. Dad had hovered like that in the doorway, hesitant, helpless, when Joey came down with chicken pox. They both knew then there was nothing Dad could do to make the miserable itching go away. There was nothing he could do now either.

"Just do what the doctor tells you, okay?" His father flashed Joey a brief smile and disappeared.

Dr. Kaminsky raised the side rails on the gurney and locked them in place. "How about I take you for a little spin?" he said, wheeling Joey down the hall.

They stopped at the elevator to wait, and the doctor took off his wire-rimmed glasses and polished them on his tie. Parrots and flamingos fluttered across the silk in a wild medley of yellow, green, orange, and pink.

"I see you're admiring my tie."

Joey coughed. "You must like tropical birds, huh?"

Dr. Kaminsky laughed. "No, but my son does. He sent this to me for my birthday."

"Oh." Joey didn't know what else to say.

The elevator dinged and the doors slid open. Dr. Kaminsky pushed the gurney inside and pressed the button for the next floor. He was silent until they reached the radiology department, where he joked with a nurse behind the reception desk for a minute and filled out several forms.

He returned and tucked a plastic clipboard next to Joey's feet. "We're in luck. They've had a cancellation, so we'll have to wait only about fifteen minutes."

Joey cleared his throat. "Dr. Kaminsky?"

"Why don't you call me Dr. K? It's shorter. A lot of my patients do. Or Gary."

"Oh, I couldn't call you that," Joey said. "Sir."

"Then Dr. K it is." He smiled. "What was it you wanted to ask me, Joey?"

"Your son, what's his name?"

"David."

"Do you talk much?"

Dr. Kaminsky folded his arms and rested them on the side rail. "Talk?"

"I mean . . ." Joey paused. This was going to be harder than he'd thought. He laced his fingers together and squeezed until his knuckles showed white through the skin. "If he told you something, would you believe him? No matter what?"

Dr. Kaminsky thought for a moment. "David's younger than you are, Joey, but in some ways you remind me of him. If he had something serious to tell me, I'd take him seriously." He tilted his head and peered at Joey. "Was there something you wanted to tell me?"

Joey shook his head.

"A lot of strange things can happen along with a

seizure," Dr. Kaminsky said. "You smelled something bad right before you passed out, didn't you?"

"Uh-huh. Like burning electric wires."

"Experiences like that are not uncommon before seizures. They're part of what's called an aura. A famous Russian writer named Dostoyevsky used to smell oranges before he had his seizures. It's completely normal."

Joey waited.

"Well, sometimes when a person has a seizure, they not only smell things, they see things as well," Dr. Kaminsky went on. "Like scenes from a dream or a movie."

"You mean a hallucination," Joey said.

"Doctors call them hallucinations, yes, but if you told me you saw something when you passed out, I wouldn't think you were crazy."

Joey flipped his head to one side, away from Dr. Kaminsky, brushing the sore spot on his cheek where the pebble had bruised it. He wanted to tell him. But what if this guy wasn't so different from his father and the sheriff after all?

Dr. Kaminsky looked at Joey. "If anything like that happened to you, you'd tell me, wouldn't you?"

Joey dropped his eyes. He couldn't do it. He couldn't tell him. Dr. K might be wearing that goofy tie his son gave him, but he was still a doctor. A grownup. The kind of person who would want a logical explanation before he'd be willing to buy a story like Joey's. But he didn't want to lie to Dr. K. "I wasn't hallucinating," he said finally.

That wasn't a lie. Joey knew that what he had experienced this afternoon in his backyard was memory, not hallucination. Something bizarre had happened to him up at Smokewater Lake two years ago. If only he knew for sure what it was.

"Okay, Joey." Dr. Kaminsky sighed. "I hope you know that if you ever need to talk to me—about anything—I'm here. And now I think they're ready for you. Don't worry—a CAT scan is noisy, but it doesn't hurt."

The nurse whisked him away. The din in his ears flared up again, whistling and popping like a bad connection on a long-distance telephone line. He wished there were a knob somewhere in his head he could adjust to filter out that annoying static and tune in to a clear signal.

Dr. K was right—a CAT scan was loud. Staccato bursts of sound assaulted his ears every few seconds like machine-gun fire. But Joey was grateful for the sound as he lay with his head inside the tunnel-like confines of the scanner. At least it drowned out the racket inside his head.

Dr. Kaminsky invited Joey and his parents into a room where a dozen oval images of his head were displayed on a backlit screen, each image a cross-section taken as if one were looking down onto the top of his skull. It gave Joey the creeps to see his head like that, practically dissected, on film.

The doctor tapped a spot near the center of one picture. "Here it is," he told them. "It's not a tumor, Mrs. Finney. Joey has a tiny fracture of the ethmoid sinus, just behind the nasal cavity."

His mother let out a sigh and put her arms around Joey, hugging him tightly. His father frowned. "So how did he fracture his sinus?"

"A CAT scan can't tell us that. Looks recent, though—the bone is just starting to heal."

Recent? Joey wondered how he could break part of his skull and not know how or when it happened.

"I don't understand," his mother said. "What does this have to do with the problems Joey's been having?"

"It's not uncommon after a serious head injury for a person to experience seizures," Dr. Kaminsky explained, "or even to suffer some memory loss. As for the runny nose, that's cerebrospinal fluid—the fluid that cushions the brain and spine. The fracture is allowing some of that fluid to leak into Joey's nose."

Joey's hands flew to his face. Brain fluid? He pinched his nostrils together.

"Is that dangerous?" his father asked.

"Not in itself," Dr. Kaminsky said, "although we do need to be careful about infection until the fracture heals. But for now I think you can take Joey home."

"No more tests?" Joey asked. "I'm done?"

"I think we've tortured you enough for one day," Dr. Kaminsky said. He removed the film from the screen and began putting it in a large manila envelope. He stopped, squinting at something on one of the pictures.

"What is it?" Joey's mother spoke sharply.

"Nothing, Mrs. Finney. Just a smudge on one of the images. I'm going to send this along to the radiologist for a look. Standard hospital procedure."

Dr. Kaminsky studied the film again for several moments before sliding it the rest of the way into the envelope.

CHAPTER SIX

From a front-page article in the October 11 edition of the
Cloudline Clarion:

LOCAL BOY'S ORDEAL PUZZLES INVESTIGATORS

The return of Rock Creek Junior High
School student Joseph Finney has not
solved the mystery of his disappearance. Local lawmen will not specu-
late publicly on what happened to
Finney, 14, of Cornish Gap, and the
boy himself has not given authorities
any clues.

Finney walked into the Minit Mart
on Hwy. 220 outside town last Monday and collapsed, 27 months after he
vanished from a family camping trip
in Jefferson National Forest. He was
hospitalized at Cloudline Regional
Medical Center for three days following his return, and so was not immediately available for questioning.
Sheriff Wade Varnadoe did interview

Finney yesterday at his home but said only, "We'll be talking to Joey again as soon as he's settled."

The sheriff confirmed reports that the FBI was assisting in the investigation. Said Varnadoe, "This case remains under local jurisdiction, but the FBI is allowing us to check all leads with their computer database of known abductors."

Joey shuffled into the kitchen in his slippers, face puffy and creased from sleep, hair sticking out in clumps. He slipped one hand into the pocket of his bathrobe and fingered a stash of tissues and a square of folded notebook paper.

"Good morning, sweetheart." Mrs. Finney gave Joey a wide smile and circled him with her arms. Her smell was familiar, reassuring—Dove soap and talcum powder. "Are you hungry?" She finished crumbling bits of toast into a bowl with soft-boiled egg and gave it to Molly, who was banging a spoon on the tray of her high chair.

Kevin snapped a bite out of his Pop Tart and buried his head in the newspaper.

"Morning, everyone." Mr. Finney walked into the kitchen. "Morning, punkin," he greeted the baby. She responded by smearing egg yolk all over her cheeks.

"Ugh, Molly," he said. "I think you missed your mouth there." He tore off a paper towel, dampened it under the faucet, and wiped her face.

"There's an article in the *Clarion* today about Joey," Kevin said.

Joey's parents looked at each other, then Mr. Finney wadded the dirty paper towel and shot it in the trash basket. "I was hoping things were going to get back to normal around here."

"What does it say?" Joey asked.

"Give me the paper, please, Kevin," Mrs. Finney said.

Kevin folded back the newspaper and continued reading. "The sheriff and the FBI want to talk to you." He eyed Joey.

"That's enough, Kevin," his mother said.

Joey's throat tightened. The FBI! He couldn't talk to them.

"It does not say that." She began combing Joey's hair with her fingers. "What can I fix you for breakfast? Sausage, bacon, pancakes, French toast?"

"You didn't offer to make *me* breakfast." Kevin glared at his brother.

"Could I just heat up a couple of frozen waffles?" Joey asked.

"Sure, honey."

His father opened the freezer compartment and reached inside. "I'll get them for you."

"I can do it."

"No, it's okay," his father said, taking two waffles out of a cardboard box and dropping them into the toaster.

Joey hung back, jamming both hands into the pockets of his bathrobe. This was weird—like staying in a hotel.

His mother set the waffles on the table with a bottle of syrup. "Come on, Joey, eat."

Joey sat down in the chair farthest from Kevin, next to Molly. Magnum lay under the high chair, tail thumping, waiting to snatch any food that dropped his way. Joey leaned down and stroked his ears.

Molly looked over at him, her round blue eyes open wide, hand frozen in the process of cramming food into her mouth. She wasn't going to start screaming again, was she? Joey braced himself.

Molly blinked, then removed a crust of toast from her mouth and held it out for Joey.

Joey looked up at his mother and saw a smile pass across her lips for an instant, like a cloud racing across the summer sky. He palmed the soggy bit of toast and wiped it into his napkin. "Gee, thanks, Molly."

Kevin jumped up and scraped his chair back from the table. "Don't play with your food, Moll." He stomped over to the counter and grabbed two mugs off a peg rack, filling them with coffee from a glass carafe. "Dad?" He offered one to his father.

"Thanks, son."

Kevin poured milk into the second mug and brought it with him to the table. He leaned across to Joey and whispered, "Can't let you have any. They say caffeine stunts your growth." Grinning like a Cheshire cat, Kevin spooned sugar into his coffee and stirred.

Joey picked up his knife and fork and concentrated on cutting his waffles into tiny squares. Mom and Dad had always said that he and Kevin were too young to drink coffee. Since when was Kevin allowed?

The kettle began to whistle and Mrs. Finney lifted it off the stove.

"Since you're taking another personal leave day from work," Mr. Finney said, "I think it would be a good idea to take Joey to school and get him registered again."

Joey jabbed his fork into a piece of waffle.

His mother dunked a teabag up and down in her mug. "Actually, I was thinking of pulling Kevin out of school for a week so that we could all get away somewhere."

"Mom!" Kevin protested. "Not in the middle of football season."

His father frowned and rubbed the bridge of his nose. "Beth, for the past two years we've all been living in a state of limbo. The sooner we can get back to some kind of routine, the better."

"The doctor said that until the fracture in his skull heals, Joey is vulnerable to infection," his mother said. "We're supposed to bring him in for antibiotics at the first sign of a cold. The last place he needs to be is school. There are always sick kids around."

"Joey's missed enough school already."

"I think we should discuss this later, Dan," Joey's mother said quietly, wrapping her teabag in a spoon and setting it on the side of the sink. "It's not going to be that simple to re-enroll him."

Joey looked back and forth between his parents. Was it their disagreeing with each other or the thought of going back to school that tied his stomach in knots?

His father pulled back the cuff of his shirt and consulted his watch. "Better get a move on, Kevin. It's time for the bus."

Kevin drained the last of his coffee and sprang up from the table. Joey followed him to the front door.

"Wait."

Kevin spun around on his heel and scowled down at Joey. "Look, shrimp, I've already missed out on a lot because of you." His voice cracked. "You're not going to make me miss my bus too."

"You don't know anything about it," Joey snapped. "Try missing out on two years of your life."

Kevin shrank back.

"You may be bigger, but I'm still older." Joey dug down in his pocket and withdrew the square of notebook paper, stapled shut along the edges. His hand was trembling. "Deliver this for me."

Kevin took the note and stared at the name HAMP DURDEN scrawled across the front. "I don't think this is such a hot idea."

"If it's too much of a strain for you, then just forget it." Joey's voice shook with anger.

"It's just, well . . ." The scowl faded from Kevin's face. "Joey, things aren't the same as they were. Stuff has changed. People have changed."

"Hamp is my best friend. You don't know him."

"Oh, yeah?" Kevin said. "All right. I'll give it to him, big brother. But if Hamp hasn't changed, if he's still such a good friend of yours, ask yourself—where was he yesterday? Why wasn't he here to welcome you home?"

CHAPTER SEVEN

Joey stared up at the big white dial of the school clock. Every sixty seconds the long hand jerked, inching backward, then leapfrogging forward to mark the passage of another minute. As if time couldn't make up its mind whether to stay in the past or come into the present.

Time. That was what it all boiled down to, wasn't it? Everything the guidance counselor was telling his mother about test scores and social maturation and grade placement.

Time had marched along without Joey these past two years. How old was he now? Twelve? That was all he could remember being. But according to his parents, he was really fourteen.

What had happened to the clock inside him? Why had it stopped ticking at the same pace as everybody else's?

"So Mrs. Finney, you can see our dilemma now, can't you?" Ms. D'Amato was saying. "Joey doesn't fit anywhere."

Joey dropped his gaze from the clock on the wall and looked sideways at his mother. A threadlike blue vein throbbed in her temple.

"Do we place him in the seventh grade, which is

where he was headed before . . ." The guidance counselor's voice trailed off, and her hands fluttered through the air, a cluster of silver bracelets clattering down one arm.

Joey balled his hands together in his lap. Seventh grade? That was a year behind Kevin. The kids who were in this year's seventh-grade class had been fourth graders the last time Joey saw them, popping bubble gum and giggling at bathroom jokes. Babies.

"Or do we place him in the ninth grade with his agemates?"

Joey tugged on the collar of his shirt, which was beginning to feel too tight. It was stuffy in Ms. D'Amato's office. The windows and door were closed and he could smell a summer's worth of dust blowing out with the overheated air from the furnace.

"But you said yourself that his test scores show that Joey is capable of working at the ninth-grade level," his mother said.

Ms. D'Amato pinched a brown leaf off a dying spider plant on the windowsill and slid behind the desk.

"Those were basic ability tests." Ms. D'Amato frowned. "They tell us that Joey is quite bright, yes. But he still needs a certain base of knowledge. The fact remains that Joey has missed two years of classroom work. We can't just plunk him down in geometry or third-year Spanish and expect him to perform at grade level. He has a lot of catching up to do."

His mother nodded. "Of course it wouldn't be easy at first. But we'd help. And Joey is intelligent—he'll catch up quickly."

Joey grinned. Score one for Mom.

"Academic considerations aren't our only concern." Ms. D'Amato shoved her bracelets back from her wrist. "There are psychosocial problems here as well. Chronologically, Joey may be fourteen—but physically? Emotionally?"

Ms. D'Amato looked at Joey for the first time during the entire conversation. He wished she hadn't. It made him feel like a bug on a pin.

"His physical development is considerably delayed. The boys at Rock Creek shower together after gym class. Have you thought this through? Can you imagine the potential for embarrassment?"

A flush of heat swept through Joey like a brushfire. He dropped his head and fumbled with his shoelaces, pretending to retie them.

"Embarrassment?" his mother said. "How do you think Joey will feel if you place him in the grade below his younger brother? How do you think he will feel when all his old friends move on to high school next year without him?"

The usual slow trickle of fluid in Joey's nose began to flood. He dug in his jeans pocket for a tissue, but he had used them all up. Ms. D'Amato would think he was starting to cry. He tilted his head back and sniffed as inconspicuously as he could. His mother glanced over, opened her purse, then squeezed Joey's hand. An oversized tissue was scrunched up in her palm. He smoothed it out and covered his nose, faking a sneeze.

"I'm sure as his mother you have Joey's best interests at heart, but it's my job to consider the facts," Ms. D'Amato said. "And my professional opinion is that he would best be placed in the seventh grade."

"No!" Joey jumped up and pounded his fists on the desk. The guidance counselor looked at him in surprise, as if she had forgotten he was there.

"I know I can do the work. I'll make up whatever I missed. But you can't put me in seventh grade. I won't go. Hamp and all my friends are in ninth grade. I belong with them."

Ms. D'Amato was silent.

Joey's mother zipped her purse shut and rose from her chair. "I think my son has just said everything that matters. Perhaps we should take this up with the principal."

Ms. D'Amato shook her head. "All right. But I want you to remember that this placement was made against my recommendation."

"Of course," his mother said.

"It might be best if you arranged for private tutoring," Ms. D'Amato went on. "And you may want to consider counseling. Of course, I'll be meeting with him on a weekly basis."

Joey swallowed hard.

"But I'm not a psychologist. After what Joey's been through, I'm sure he has a lot of issues to deal with."

Joey's mother put her arm around his shoulder. "Joey is already under a doctor's care. Our family will do whatever it takes to help him pick up his life where he left off."

The two women's eyes met.

"Stop by my office first thing Monday morning and pick up your class card, Joey," the guidance counselor directed. "We'll schedule our first session then."

Joey spiked his used tissue in the wastebasket and as he and his mother headed into the hallway, he pulled the door shut behind them. "Thanks, Mom."

"Ms. D'Amato was right about one thing, Joey," his mother said. "This won't be easy."

"Yeah, I guess I'll have a lot of homework to do," Joey said, gazing at the green metal lockers that lined the hall. Ms. D'Amato would probably assign him a locker on Monday. No more sitting at an assigned desk with the same teacher all day. He'd be changing classes and memorizing the combination to his first locker. Maybe it would be close to Hamp's. "It'll be worth it."

His mother studied him. "Homework will be part of it, but you have to prepare yourself—"

Joey interrupted her. He heard a girl say "Hamp," and then an admiring laugh. He turned to look.

A freckle-faced boy with coppery hair, dressed in chinos and a pink Oxford shirt, cruised down the hall in a flotilla of other kids. Smiling and talking, he hitched a backpack over one shoulder and twined hands with the girl beside him.

Joey raised one arm above his head and waved. "Hamp!"

The boy glanced up at the sound of his name but didn't answer or wave back. His smile faded.

For a split second Joey wondered if he'd made a mistake. Hamp had always been a little on the pudgy side, but this kid, though squarely built, had no trace of fat. Pink sleeves were rolled up over broad forearms, like those of a pitcher or tennis player.

Also, Hamp hated girls. The Hamp that Joey remembered wouldn't be caught dead holding hands with one. Joey blinked. Was that Amy Showalter? Wearing lip gloss and stockings and a—Joey's mind stumbled over the word—a bra?

Joey looked down at his own thin arms and was suddenly conscious of how high and girlish his voice had sounded when he called out to Hamp. Noise whined in his ears and he began to feel a little dizzy.

Hamp stared across the hall and whispered something behind his hand to the knot of kids with him. Heads turned, and a burst of laughter erupted from the group. Then Hamp tugged on Amy's hand and slipped into the classroom, never acknowledging Joey at all.

Joey felt as if the breath had been knocked out of him, as if someone had just slammed him into a stone wall at fifty miles an hour.

Was this the same Hamp who had tossed Joey a thousand fly balls to help him make the outfield on the baseball team?

"Can we go home now, Mom?"

"Oh, Joey," his mother sighed, squeezing his shoulder. "I'm sorry."

He shook off her hand. "I just want to go home."

Joey watched as a tiny envelope flashed at the bottom of the computer screen.

"Looks like I've got e-mail," his mother said.

There was a loud thunk on the ceiling above their heads.

"Molly should be exhausted by now," Joey's mother said in exasperation. "She's had lunch, and Mrs. Nuttall said she never went down for her morning nap. She should sleep for a couple of hours at least."

Maybe his little sister wasn't tired, but Joey was. He felt hollow with fatigue, and a dull headache was starting behind his nose. He plopped down on the couch and let his eyes travel around the living room.

His parents had made some changes while he was gone. They had pushed the couch away from the wall to make room for a long table with folding metal legs. The computer and printer and a photocopier sat on that table, along with cardboard boxes filled with blank paper and several thick telephone directories. The large painting of an English fox hunt that used to hang over the couch had been replaced with a bulletin board. His face was tacked all over it, grinning from flyers and posters that read MISSING CHILD.

"What is all this stuff?" he asked.

"I told you," his mother said, "no one in Cornish Gap forgot you. We did everything we could to find you—put up posters, mailed out flyers, even started our own news-group on the Internet."

There was another loud thump from the ceiling, and

Molly screeched. His mother ran her hands through her hair. "I really need to get some work done this afternoon." Sighing, she pushed back from the table and headed upstairs.

Joey got up from the couch and walked over to the computer. He wondered if his mother was still receiving e-mail messages about him and his disappearance.

Scooting the mouse around on its blue foam pad, he clicked on the envelope icon and the first message appeared on the screen. It was addressed to his mother from one of her co-workers at the college library. He scrolled through the next two messages. They were about work too. They would probably all be about work.

He clicked the mouse one more time. The next message was not for his mother at all. It was addressed to him.

Message: 4
From: Albert Einstein
<e.glass@bmsc.edu>
Date: Fri Oct 11 13:27:09
To: Joseph Finney
Subject: Lost time

Welcome back, Finney. I've been trying to call, but your line is always busy, or somebody answers and asks me to leave a message. This isn't exactly the kind of thing I want to get into with your folks on the phone, you know? Guess you don't know—

that's kind of the point, isn't it? If that rag of a newspaper got it right, you don't remember what happened to you. I think I can help you figure it out. Want to find out more? Reply to the Glass Man.

Joey heard his mother's footsteps on the stairs. He punched the print button, then erased the message from the screen.

CHAPTER EIGHT

Friday, October. 11, 2:25 P.M.

\<e.glass@bmsc.edu\>

Joey picked up the phone in his parents' bedroom and called Burnt Mountain State College. That was what "bmsc" stood for in the e-mail message he had received.

At least the rules of computer addresses hadn't changed while he'd been gone. The letters after the @ told him where the message came from. The letters before the @ told him who had sent it—not Albert Einstein, but someone named E. Glass.

"How many?" Joey asked the operator, grabbing a pencil. "Could you give me all of them, please?"

There were three E. Glasses at the college. Joey sighed and studied the list.

1. Edwina Glass, dean of students
2. Elgin Glass, Classics professor
3. Ethan Glass, a freshman living in a dormitory called Plowman Hall.

Joey thought he could rule out Dean Glass and the Classics professor. The freshman was his best bet. Ethan Glass. Probably some nerd with a calculator strapped to his belt and his shirt buttoned up to his chin.

Joey hesitated. Maybe sending crank e-mail was this nerd's idea of a joke. Hilarious. Just like the time when Joey was eight that two sixth graders convinced him his fairy godmother was leaving notes in a hollow tree. One of the notes told him to eat twelve peppercorns or his godmother would die.

"You're in third grade now," his father had said after Joey got sick trying to chew the bitter spice. "I thought you were big enough to know when someone was pulling your leg."

No one was going to make a fool of him again. But what if the message wasn't a joke? What if this Ethan Glass really knew something that the sheriff and Joey's parents and Dr. Kaminsky didn't?

It was a risk. This Glass guy could be a jerk, or worse. But Joey needed to know how he had lost the past two years. He was surprised how much he needed to know: more than he cared about some geek making him look like an idiot, more than he cared about the trouble he'd surely get into for running off to meet this guy. It was weird to think he had done things he couldn't remember. It made him feel uneasy, naked almost, as if he were standing in front of a roomful of people with his fly unzipped.

He tiptoed downstairs and peeked into the living room. Good—Mom was still clacking away at the computer, her back to the door. Maybe he could sneak out. If he hurried, he could ride over to the campus, find Ethan

Glass, and get home before she called him for dinner.

Joey pushed open the metal fire door at the top of the stairwell and turned into a long hallway lined with rooms. Music blasted through the air, rock and country clashing in a battle of radios and stereo systems. A guy who wore nothing but a towel cinched around his waist slid into the hall. Dripping water on the floor, he let out a loud belch.

Joey pressed one shoulder against the wall and walked to the end of the hall. The only door in the dorm that was shut was 417, the room number that the operator had given him. Joey wiped his palms on his jeans and knocked. The door swung open and he heard the sound of classical music—horns and violins and oboes.

A tall young woman stood at the door, wearing a loose blouse over a long gauze skirt. Auburn hair fell in corkscrews down her back.

Suddenly Joey couldn't think of a thing to say.

"Come on in," the girl said, stepping inside. "Ethan, I think this might be him."

A thick sheet of gray foam padded the back of the door. Soundproofing, Joey guessed, since he hadn't been able to hear the classical music out in the hall.

A black shade was pulled down over the window, a poster of a wild-haired Einstein stapled to the back. IMAGINATION IS MORE IMPORTANT THAN KNOWLEDGE, the poster read. Books were piled on the windowsill beneath it. Joey glanced at some of the titles: *Sightings*, *The Edge of Reality*, *Uninvited Guests*, and *The Inner Reaches of Outer*

Space. Odd collection. He drew back a half-step toward the door.

Computers dominated the room. Ever-changing kaleidoscopes of color marched across three different monitors. Diskettes and printouts were scattered everywhere. Slumped in a chair staring intently at the pattern on one of the screens was a slight young man with gray-tinted glasses and a ponytail who Joey assumed was Ethan Glass. He balled up an empty bag of Fritos and tossed it to the floor.

"Shut the door," he said. "That noise is polluting my Bach."

Ethan dragged his eyes away from the computer screen and jutted his head forward, looking at Joey for the first time. He slid his glasses up the bridge of his nose.

"You're Finney?" He fished through a muddle of papers on his desk and came up with a flyer. Joey recognized it from his mother's bulletin board in the living room.

Ethan squinted at the photo and compared it to Joey. His sallow face lit up. "See what I meant, Ariel?"

"Don't treat him like a lab rat," she said.

"Sorry, man," Ethan apologized. "I just had to see for myself."

"Forgive us," the girl said. "There's so much we want to talk about. But we're forgetting our manners. I'm Ariel DeWitt. Introduce yourself, Ethan."

"Since he successfully tracked me down, he already knows who I am," Ethan said. "Put it here, man." He offered his hand to Joey and they shook. His grip was firm and steady, stronger than Joey had expected. "Delighted to make your acquaintance—overjoyed, to be precise."

Joey remembered how Hamp and the other kids had shunned him at school. Was it only this morning? "I don't seem to have that effect on many people lately."

Ethan plucked a leftover Frito off his sweatshirt and popped the corn chip in his mouth. "Just blow them off. They're clueless. If they had any idea—"

"Aren't you getting ahead of yourself?" Ariel interrupted. "I thought that's why we wanted to meet Joey. To check out these ideas of yours."

She sat on the bed and gestured to the mattress beside her. "Have a seat."

He sat down next to her, careful to leave a space between them. Up close she smelled like apples.

"Do you know what happened to me?" he asked.

Ethan pulled his chair up to the bed. "I've got a theory."

Joey sighed. A theory. Is that all Ethan had?

"The *Clarion* said you were fourteen," Ethan said. "Is that true?"

"Yeah." Joey lifted his chin.

"Well, last week Ari was finishing her shift at the hospital."

"I work there part-time in the lab," she said.

"Ari's premed—going to get her M.D. and Ph.D., be a hotshot neurobiologist one day."

"Not if I don't pass physics." She shook her head.

"What does any of this have to do with me?" Joey asked.

"Ari overheard some of the nurses talking about you. She knew I'd be interested." Ethan inclined his head toward the window with its poster of Einstein and the jumbled pile of books. "Said you'd been missing for two years and hadn't grown at all since the day you left."

Joey's face began to burn. "So?"

"So that ties in with some ideas I've been kicking around." Ethan tilted his chair back and crossed a pair of black hightop sneakers on the edge of the bed. "Ari's here to make sure I don't go off the deep end. That I consider every possible medical explanation for why you don't look any older. In return, I'm going to make sure she aces physics."

"I don't know which is going to be harder," Ariel said. "Ethan doesn't want to listen to anything I have to say. He is so hyped up about the possibility that—well, it's your theory, Ethan. You tell him."

Ethan leaned forward. "I wonder if somehow you might have been caught up in a distortion of spacetime."

Joey snorted. "That's it? That's what you wanted to tell me? I think you've watched one too many reruns of *Star Trek*."

"Hear me out," Ethan said. "Einstein showed us that time is elastic. It's not the same everywhere in the universe. It stretches and shrinks."

"I've read about Einstein."

"Then you know that how fast or slow time goes depends on how fast or slow you are moving through space. The faster you move, the slower time goes."

Joey looked at Ariel. Was she buying this? Ariel raised one eyebrow and shrugged.

"You wouldn't notice anything different," Ethan explained. "But if you'd been traveling at the speed of light, you'd find that a trip that seemed to take only a few days had lasted years back here on earth."

"I thought nothing could travel at the speed of light," Joey said. "Einstein said so."

"But what if Einstein was wrong?" Ethan asked. Behind the gray lenses of his glasses, a light shone in his eyes. "What if some unimaginable extraterrestrial technology made it possible? You wouldn't have grown or aged."

"Ethan, we've been through this before." Ariel frowned. "Joey's failure to develop in the past two years suggests a couple of things—a hormonal deficiency maybe, something wrong with his pituitary gland. It doesn't justify the kind of leap you're making here."

Joey barely heard her. Extraterrestrial, that's what Ethan had said. "What are you getting at?" he asked.

"Stick with me, Finney. I did some research on your disappearance," Ethan continued. "I pulled up all the back issues of the *Clarion*. What was interesting to me was what they didn't find. There were no footprints other than yours, no tire tracks, no fibers snagged on bushes—nothing."

The hair rose on the back of Joey's neck.

"Next I cruised the Web and logged on to a UFO newsgroup, and man, I hit the mother lode."

"UFO?" Joey started to squirm. Next Ethan would hand

him a couple of peppercorns and tell him to chew.

"Watch it, Ethan," Ariel said, glancing at Joey's face.

"Starting the March before you disappeared, there was a sudden rash of UFO sightings in the Alleghenies. No home videos of little green men or flying saucers or anything like that, just lights in the sky. There were the usual official denials and explanations—satellites, weather balloons, meteor showers."

"Is there a point to all this?" Joey asked.

"I made a map. It's around here somewhere." Ethan searched unsuccessfully through the mess. "I plotted the locations of every report for those months. Want to know what I found?"

"No." Joey could guess what Ethan was about to say.

"Jefferson National Forest was at the center of all the UFO activity—and Smokewater Lake was dead in the middle."

Joey tried to laugh. "Right. You're not telling me you think I was . . . ?"

"I know I sound like a reporter for the *National Enquirer*," Ethan said, "but yeah, I think you were abducted by aliens."

Joey jumped up. "I'm going home now."

Ariel squeezed his hand. "It's okay, Joey. It's just a theory. It doesn't mean it really happened that way."

"Think, Finney," Ethan persisted. "And then look in the mirror."

Joey didn't need a mirror.

"The reason you don't look any older than when you

disappeared, Finney," Ethan pressed on, "is that you're not. Fourteen years may have passed here on Earth since the day you were born, but the old bod's only twelve."

Joey looked down at himself and thought of Kevin: thirteen years old, supposedly a whole year younger than Joey, but deep-voiced and a head taller.

"Can you remember anything at all about what happened to you?" Ariel asked.

Joey scratched his nose and a flake of skin peeled off in his fingers. Five days ago he'd been in the hospital. When had he gotten this sunburn?

Two years ago—at the lake.

"Shut up!" he yelled. "I don't want to hear any more."

Joey fled downstairs, ignoring Ariel's and Ethan's voices echoing behind him. He unlocked his bike from the rack in front of the dorm and raced through the streets as the sun set over the mountains.

He didn't stop until Sheriff Varnadoe pulled him over, blue lights flashing on the patrol car.

CHAPTER NINE

Friday, October. 11, 6:00 P.M.

The sheriff hoisted Joey's bicycle with one arm and swung it in the back of the Chevy Blazer that served as a county patrol car. The rear gate wouldn't close all the way, so he had to rummage around looking for a piece of rope to tie it down.

In the front seat, Joey stared through the windshield. The dark bulk of Burnt Mountain brooded over the town of Cornish Gap, casting shadows that seemed to bleed out of the ground itself. In the west, the last rays of daylight ignited a swirl of clouds, streaks of charcoal and ash smoldering with red.

Joey held his breath. That was what the sky had looked like the night he disappeared. Brighter maybe, but still the same spiraling pattern of colors, like a whirlpool or tornado or . . .

A hole being tunneled in the sky.

Think.

That was all he could remember. Just the circle rising out of the lake, and the vortex spinning over his head, and then—nothing.

No spaceship, and no journey to the stars, and nobody who looked like anything from *Star Wars* or *E.T.*

The car sagged as Sheriff Varnadoe slid behind the steering wheel. "You buckled up, son?"

"Yes, sir."

Joey glanced sideways at the man. Whatever trouble he was in, he wished the sheriff would just drive him home. It was getting dark, and there were too many windows in the patrol car, too much exposed glass. The first few stars were waking. Joey didn't want to be out in the open.

Why not? What was he afraid of if he didn't believe what Ethan Glass had told him?

Joey rubbed his finger along the bridge of his nose and again felt the raw new skin where a two-year-old sunburn was just now flaking off.

"You got your mama worked up all over again," the sheriff was saying. "She thinks you went and disappeared on her a second time. Why didn't you tell her where you were going?"

Joey didn't answer.

The springs in the seat creaked as Sheriff Varnadoe shifted his weight and turned to face Joey. "Is this what happened the first time? Did you run away then, too?"

Joey whipped his head back and forth. "I never ran away!"

"I didn't think so." A smile flickered across the sheriff's mouth. "Not too many runaways take off on their bikes. But I had to ask."

"I was just tired of being cooped up inside today, that's all," Joey said.

"Sure you were. But your folks have been through a

lot. Next time let them know you're leaving. Are we straight on that, son?"

Joey nodded.

"Mind telling me where you've been?"

Joey bit his lip to stifle a panicky laugh. What did the sheriff want to know: where he had been just now, or where he had been the past two years? He didn't want to answer one question and he couldn't answer the other.

"Look at me, son."

Reluctantly, Joey met Sheriff Varnadoe's gaze.

"I know you remember something." The sheriff rubbed his hand over his face. "I was hoping we could clear this up right here, just between you and me. There's an FBI agent up in Washington who's itching to come down here and question you. Talk to me, son. I don't think I can keep him at bay much longer."

The sheriff stared hard at Joey, peering into his eyes as if he could see straight through to his soul.

Joey blinked and turned away, pressing his forehead against the window. Even if he wanted to, what could he tell the sheriff? Did he really believe he had been kidnapped by aliens who knew how to outrun light and stop time?

"Look in the mirror," Ethan had said.

A single drop of sweat crawled down the back of Joey's neck.

He didn't want to believe any of it, but part of him wondered. What if Ethan was right? Ethan's explanation was the only one strange enough to account for all the bizarre things that had happened to Joey.

A sunburn that took two years to heal. Brain fluid leaking out of his nose. A maelstrom of light rising out of Smokewater Lake. Looking twelve when he was supposed to be fourteen.

Was it possible? Had he been abducted by aliens?

Joey looked over at the sheriff. This was a man who believed only in the kind of evidence he could take to court. There was nothing Joey could say.

And if he couldn't tell Sheriff Varnadoe, there was no way he could tell someone from the FBI. They wouldn't believe the truth, but they wouldn't believe his silence either. No matter what he said, he would lose.

Joey twisted his fingers together and stared out into the deepening night. Venus blazed like a watchful eye in the darkness, lying in wait.

He was afraid.

Joey's fingers hovered over the keypad of the telephone in his parents' bedroom. Muffled voices drifted up to him. He was safe for the moment—everybody else was down in the den, glued to Friday night programs on the television set. He glanced back over his shoulder, then punched in Hamp's number.

The phone was picked up on the second ring. "May I say who is calling?" the Durdens' housekeeper asked.

Joey scrambled for a name. "Brett Howell." Joey had seen Brett this morning at school, bobbing along in Hamp's wake, wearing the navy-and-green team shirt of the Rock Creek Highlanders. Surely Hamp would take a call from Brett. Joey wasn't so certain Hamp would come to the phone for him.

But Joey had to talk to Hamp. He had to tell somebody what was going on.

Joey waited, his eyes darting nervously back and forth to the doorway, while the housekeeper summoned Hamp to the phone.

A husky voice, though not as deep as Kevin's, sounded in Joey's ear. "Hey, Brett. You're worse than a girl, yammering on the phone all day. We hung up less than twenty minutes ago."

"It's me, Hamp. Joey."

There was silence on the other end of the line.

"I guess you weren't expecting to see me today in school, huh?"

"What do you want?"

"Didn't you get my note?" Joey heard his voice rising, but he couldn't stop himself.

"Yeah. Kevin gave it to me."

"Well?" Dad's meatloaf began to burn in Joey's stomach. This phone call was a mistake. But he still hoped he could find the right thing to say, some button he could push that would wake up the old Hamp, the one who had once been his best friend.

"I've got to go now, Joey. I've got a date with Amy Showalter tonight."

"Wait!" Joey begged. "Do you remember anything strange about that night up at Smokewater Lake?"

"The night you disappeared?" For the first time Joey heard a hint of interest in Hamp's voice.

"Can you keep a secret?" Joey didn't wait for an answer. "I've just talked to someone who thinks—get this—that I wasn't just missing." He took a deep breath. "He thinks I was yanked out of time. A few days for me was two years back here on Earth."

There was a strangled snort on the other end of the line. "Back here on Earth? Where else is there that you could have been—thumbing a ride with aliens?"

"Crazy, huh?" Joey laughed weakly. "The doctor says I have amnesia, but you know, it doesn't feel like I've forgotten two whole years. It feels like they never happened to me in the first place. Like I fell asleep next to you in the tent up at the lake and woke up the next morning at the hospital."

"You're serious, aren't you?" There was an edge creep in Hamp's voice. "Who was this guy? What else did he tell you?"

"Oh, just some computer jock," Joey said. "I'm not saying I believe him. But there *is* some strange stuff happening to me."

Hamp pounced. "What kind of strange stuff?"

Joey felt the familiar draining sensation in his nose and wiped it with a tissue. "For one thing, my nose is always running. The doctor says it's spinal fluid leaking out through a crack in one of my skull bones."

"Gross," Hamp said.

"But the weirdest thing is—well, you saw me. I don't

look any older. Even the doctors can't figure out why."

"So you believe this dweeb's story?"

Joey hesitated. It didn't feel as good as he imagined it would to confide in Hamp. "I didn't say that. I just wanted to talk it over with you."

"Sure," Hamp said. "Maybe later. My father's waiting to drive Amy and me to the movies."

"Okay," Joey said. "I'll be back in school on Monday. We could sit together in class."

"Yeah, right. Got to go." He hung up.

Joey shoulders sagged. Had he done the right thing?

"You're supposed to be in your room."

Joey jumped guiltily and whirled around. Kevin lounged in the doorway, arms across his chest. Magnum sidled in behind him.

"Dad sentenced you to solitary confinement. I wonder what he'd say if he knew you were using the phone."

Joey placed the handset back in its cradle. "And you're going to rush right down and tell him, aren't you?"

Kevin smirked.

Joey pushed past him and stalked down the hall to his room. He plopped down on the captain's bed, which was raised up on two rows of pullout drawers. Magnum jumped up beside Joey and made himself comfortable, his great head lolling between his paws.

Following close on Joey's heels, Kevin entered the room a moment later.

"Stay out," Joey commanded.

Kevin backed up and made a great show of lining the

toes of his shoes up against the threshold. "I wouldn't presume to enter the Joseph Patrick Finney Memorial Museum. Mom dusted and vacuumed and polished in here every week while you were gone. Of course, *I* was expected to clean my room myself."

Joey rose off the bed and planted himself in front of Kevin. "Come off it. We've always been expected to clean our rooms. I just wasn't here to do mine." He poked his finger in Kevin's chest. "What's your problem? Ever since I came home from the hospital, you've been on my case."

Kevin poked Joey back. "It's just nice to see Mr. Perfect in trouble for a change, that's all."

"I never said I was perfect."

"Like you weren't always getting straight A's and taking out the trash without having to be asked. Boy Scout, altar boy, Little League champ. You were always the one Dad bragged about."

They stared at each other without speaking.

Finally Kevin asked, "Who were you talking to on the phone?"

"Why do you want to know? So you can tattle to Dad?"

"You called Hamp!" Kevin grimaced. "After what he did to you in school today?"

"He probably didn't recognize me at first, that's all."

"Don't make excuses for him," Kevin said. "You look exactly the same as you did the last time he saw you. What's not to recognize?"

Joey clamped his teeth together.

"Hampton Durden is the biggest jerk in the entire

school," Kevin went on. "So his dad owns the papermill—big deal. He didn't brag about it when he was a kid, but he's full of himself now."

Joey gripped the door and started to swing it shut, shoving Kevin out of the room. "I'm in solitary, remember? Get out."

Kevin retreated down the hall. Joey locked the door behind him and was left alone with an oppressive silence. He could no longer hear the comforting drone of the television and his parents' voices from downstairs, just the dog snuffling on the bed. The stillness made him more aware of the ever-present static in his ears. It sounded rough and scratchy, like an old record.

Joey prowled the room, restless as a circus animal in a cage. When he first came back from the hospital, his room seemed welcoming, secure. Everything was the way he had left it—the Baltimore Orioles poster on the wall, the H. G. Wells and Michael Crichton books on the shelf, the Legos on his desk.

But now the room felt like a trap. Magnum watched Joey pace back and forth from his perch on the bed, his ears pricked forward.

The night sky pressed against the window, seeming to bulge in through the glass. Joey could see the cold light of a million stars glaring at him from the blackness. He ran to the window and pulled down the blind.

The noise in his ears grew louder, the static dissipating. Joey cocked his head to one side. What a relief. It was as if he had finally succeeded in tuning the knob on a cheap transistor radio into a clear station. He could almost hear music in the background.

He blocked his ears with his fingers. It was music, or something like it—not a song or a melody, but more like wind chimes tinkling tunelessly in the breeze.

Then, faint but distinct, he heard the words *the door in the lake, the door in the lake—come,* over and over again.

CHAPTER TEN

Monday, October 14, 7:00 A.M.

"Sorry," the message on the computer read. "You have no mail." Sighing, Joey switched off the power and the screen went blank.

Come on, Ethan, Joey thought. Please check your e-mail.

Joey had been trying all weekend to contact Ethan on the computer, sneaking into the living room whenever he could: two A.M. Saturday morning, Sunday after Mass while Mom was planting tulip and daffodil bulbs out front and Dad and Kevin were raking leaves.

But now it was Monday morning, and still there had been no reply.

Joey pressed his hands over his ears. Nothing. So far he had heard the voice only at night, every night since Friday, drilling the same words into his brain:

The door in the lake, the door in the lake—come.

When he finally managed to fall asleep, the words invaded his dreams. But by morning the voice was gone. All that remained was a whooshing sound, like air blowing from an electric fan or the rush of a distant stream. A faint, high-pitched hum whined in the background, as if a gnat were buzzing in his ear.

Was this what it was like to go crazy—hearing a voice that wasn't your own inside your head? It even had a strange accent, a staccato, stilted cadence of speech, as if it were not being spoken by a person but synthesized by a machine—like the robotic voices in the monorail at the airport.

Was this what those freaky people featured in *National Enquirer* stories heard when aliens spoke?

Joey's nerves tingled, shivers rippling down his spine. Either he was going crazy or Ethan Glass was right. Neither possibility was very reassuring.

His father's voice startled him. "Shake a leg, Joey. The bus will be here any minute."

Joey turned around to find his father standing in the archway that separated the living room from the front hall. Dad's whole face was lit up.

He cupped his hand around one of Joey's shoulders and gave it a quick squeeze. "Today's the big day. Have you got everything you need?"

Kevin skulked in the hall. "Jeez, all you have to do is show up for school and suddenly you're Mr. Perfect again," he muttered.

Dad was acting as if he'd forgotten all about Sheriff Varnadoe bringing Joey home Friday night, and about banishing him to his room.

Joey's mother came downstairs, balancing Molly on one hip and buttoning her into a pair of corduroy overalls. At the bottom of the stairs she looked at Joey. "Are you sure you're ready for this?" She reached out and brushed his hair off his forehead. "You look so pale, and you didn't touch a bite of your breakfast. Do you want me to drop you off at school today?"

Kevin rolled his eyes.

Joey's father crossed his arms and frowned. At that moment he looked more like a judge, or a teacher handing out exam papers, than the traffic engineer he was.

Joey looked at his father, then at Kevin. "No thanks, Mom," he said. "Nobody's parents drive them to school."

The frown evaporated from his father's face. "See, Beth? He's got nothing to be nervous about, do you, sport?"

Joey guessed he had passed the test.

Kevin yanked the door open and marched outside, slamming his backpack against the porch rail as he pounded down the steps.

"See you later," Joey said. He shouldered his backpack, took a deep breath, and followed Kevin down the sidewalk.

The school bus pulled up, grinding gears and belching diesel fumes, just as Joey reached the corner stop at the end of Laurel Street. Kevin barged on ahead of him.

The usual chatter ceased as soon as Joey stepped aboard. Thirty pairs of eyes trailed him, heads swiveling silently as he moved down the aisle. Kevin was already sitting next to Travis, but several kids who were sitting alone scooted toward the aisle as Joey approached. Finally he turned around and dropped in the empty seat behind the bus driver. No one ever sat there.

The day skidded downhill from there. Ms. D'Amato was waiting for him in the hall as soon as he entered the building. "Welcome back, Joey," she said, steering him toward her office. "This will only take a minute."

An overpowering school smell followed them down the hall, a mixture of floor wax, copier fluid, and the musty odor of old textbooks, all overlaid with the stubborn aroma of thirty years' worth of the cafeteria's canned peas.

Ms. D'Amato slipped a key out of her skirt pocket and unlocked her office. She did not invite Joey inside, so he stood awkwardly at the entrance as she made her way to her desk.

"All the available lockers were assigned even before school began last month," the guidance counselor said. "You've got a backpack. I'm afraid you'll have to carry all your books with you."

Joey slumped against the door frame. No locker? He stared over his shoulder into the hall. A boy and girl were studying a poster for the upcoming Halloween dance, wrapped around each other like pretzels.

Joey looked closer and blinked. Was that Carrie Beth Shelnutt and Dwayne Billue? Carrie Beth, who used to brag in elementary school about how long she could go without combing her hair, with a perm and purple eye shadow. Baby-faced Dwayne with dark fuzz over his lip, the ghost of a mustache.

Joey touched his own lip. It was as smooth as his baby sister's.

Ms. D'Amato handed him a pale green card. "Here is

your class schedule."

Joey ran his eyes over the list: geometry, English, physical science, world history, Spanish, health, and gym. He hadn't fully realized how much catching up he had to do.

"It's a demanding schedule," Ms. D'Amato said. "So I think you'll be relieved that I decided to place you in Spanish I."

"With seventh graders?" Joey asked.

"You're in a ninth-grade homeroom, and all your other classes are with ninth graders, too." Ms. D'Amato leaned closer, her earrings dangling in Joey's face. "But you'd have no hope of making it in an advanced-level Spanish class when you don't know a word of the language."

But I do, Joey wanted to say. Taco, tortilla, buenos dias Señorita D'Amato. But it was probably better to keep his mouth shut.

She tore another dead leaf off the spider plant on her windowsill. "Also, you'll note that you don't have music on Friday with everybody else. You'll meet with me instead."

Joey checked his schedule. It was peppered with land mines. Ms. D'Amato on Fridays. P.E. on Tuesdays and Thursdays—that meant showering in the locker room after class.

A bell shrilled.

"That was the late bell," Ms. D'Amato said. "I'll inform your homeroom teacher you were with me. You've got four minutes to get to your first-period class."

Joey backed out into the hall. Where was he supposed

to be now? Monday, first period—that was geometry. He tightened his grip on the strap of his backpack and started to jog toward the math/science wing. That was a mistake. It earned him a reprimand from the vice principal about running in the hall.

Every class was the same. Teachers assigned him a desk and gave him piles of make-up work. His backpack grew heavier and heavier, digging into his shoulder. A few kids said hello, but after that the conversation died. Joey didn't know what to say to them. Their lives had moved on; his had stalled up at Smokewater Lake. They no longer had anything in common.

By the time he got to history, his last class before lunch, Joey couldn't wait for freedom. He counted the minutes, waiting for the bell as the hands of the school clock jerked toward the lunch hour.

"Mr. Finney!"

Joey stiffened and turned toward the blackboard where Mr. Beatty, his history teacher, had stopped in the act of writing an outline of the Punic Wars.

"There is no clock-watching in my class," the teacher said, shaking a piece of chalk at Joey. "For fifty minutes a day your time is my time. It belongs to me. And I will not tolerate you wasting my time by worshipping the clock when you should be listening to me. Do I make myself understood?"

Joey gulped. "Yes, Mr. Beatty."

"Excellent. Since I didn't get to finish my lecture to-day, I'll expect an oral report from you tomorrow on the causes of the war."

The lunch bell rang. Joey shut his notebook in a daze. An oral report! He already had hours of homework to do. He shifted his backpack off his left shoulder, which was beginning to ache, and shuffled out of the room after all the other kids had left.

"Joseph." It was Mr. Beatty again.

"Yes, sir?"

"May I inquire why you transport all your books in that knapsack instead of storing them in your locker?"

"I don't have a locker. Ms. D'Amato said they ran out."

"Did she?" Mr. Beatty removed his glasses and wiped the lenses with a handkerchief. "Why don't you keep your bag here then? You can pick it up after lunch."

Joey brightened. "Thanks." He rushed off to the cafeteria, walking fast but being careful not to run. Maybe now he'd have a chance to talk to Hamp.

By the time Joey reached the lunchroom Hamp was already seated, surrounded by Amy and Brett and the rest of their crowd. Joey saw Kevin with Travis at a table across the room. It was almost the end of eighth-grade lunch period.

Joey slid his tray along the metal serving shelf and bumped it against the one in front of his, waiting impatiently for the line to move. The smell of barbecued chicken and Tater Tots made him queasy.

Joey paid the cashier and walked over to Hamp's table. Out of the corner of his eye he could see Kevin getting up and clearing the remains of his lunch into the trash.

Hamp's table was crowded but not full. There was one empty seat, next to Brett Howell. As Joey headed toward that space, Brett shielded his mouth with his hand, leaned over to Hamp, and whispered something. Brett glanced at Joey and snickered.

Hamp's cheeks and the tips of his ears turned pink.

Joey stopped where he stood, feeling the heat rise in his own face.

Maybe Brett was making fun of him, but Hamp was worse. Hamp was embarrassed, ashamed to admit that he had once been best friends with a runt like Joey.

Joey turned on his heel and stumbled over to the first empty seat he could find.

Joey sleepwalked through the afternoon. Hamp was no longer his friend. He didn't think he had any friends anymore.

On the way home Joey sat in the same spot on the bus, heaving his backpack onto the seat beside him to fill what he was sure would be an empty space.

Kevin and Travis boarded the bus together, but Kevin sat down by himself behind Joey.

"You two have a fight?" Joey asked.

"Nope," Kevin said. "I just wanted to sit up front. Bad day, huh?"

Joey shrugged.

"I saw what happened in the cafeteria."

"So?" Joey turned around and stared at his brother.

"So nothing. I told you Hamp was a jerk, that's all." Kevin's gray eyes were steady.

Joey faced forward and rested his head against the window. He was too tired to talk, too tired to think.

The bus lumbered down Buchanan Street past the park. Hickory trees lined both sides of the street, spaced at regular intervals. The afternoon sun slanted through the trees, and as the bus drove by shafts of gold flickered off and on like a strobe light, flashing in Joey's eyes.

The bus, the trees, the street all started to spin, whirling around Joey as if he were standing in the center of a merry-go-round. He smelled the burning-wire stench of ozone and felt all the muscles of his body go limp.

The world went dark. From far away he heard Kevin saying, "Joey, Joey. Are you okay?"

CHAPTER ELEVEN

Tuesday, July 5, 1:36 A.M.
Two years earlier

His stomach plunged, like a nighthawk swooping after its prey, and the ground fell away beneath Joey's feet. Something stiff bristled against his ankles. He glanced down and saw the top of a pine tree receding swiftly into the darkness.

Hail Mary, full of grace . . .

Joey hurtled through the air, sucked upward in a nauseating spiral like a leaf in a whirlwind. Smokewater Lake churned a hundred feet below him. The squat log walls of the Forest Service latrine dwindled, then disappeared in the ever-increasing distance.

Joey flailed his arms and legs, grabbing at the air, but there was nothing to hold on to. His bones went as rubbery and weak as the chicken leg his teacher had soaked in vinegar during fourth-grade science. He felt as if he was about to plummet down the first big drop on a roller coaster without a track beneath him. There was nothing holding him up. He could fall to earth any second.

Don't look down.

He squinted up into the blaze of colors gyrating above him, a kaleidoscope of blue and red and yellow sparking and reeling in the night sky, tunneling a hole through the clouds to the stars beyond. Blinded, he shut his eyes and covered them with his hands.

Joey spun higher and higher. After a while the air thickened, taking on substance, as if the molecules of nitrogen and oxygen were congealing. Joey felt that he was being pushed up against a flexible barrier of some kind, a tough elastic membrane that stretched but would not tear. Like a piece of plastic wrap, it molded tightly around his nose and mouth, making it hard for him to breathe.

As Joey was pulled upward, the sense of pressure increased, becoming painful. The harder he was pulled against it, the more the membrane seemed to resist. It felt as if a giant vacuum cleaner was trying to suck Joey through a pinhole. He didn't know whether he would suffocate or break apart first.

Then the tension suddenly gave way, the membrane burst, and Joey knew he had been propelled through to the other side.

But the other side of what?

He was lying on something solid. A puff of air blew softly against his skin, and Joey heard a musical sound like the tinkling of wind chimes. Like wind chimes, but different. There was something purposeful about this sound, a rhythm and order that was totally unlike the random tones of chimes in a breeze. Joey listened hard. Was he hearing a pattern, the same sequence of notes repeated over and over?

It was almost as if something alive was making the

sound.

Holy Mary, Mother of God, pray for us sinners, now . . .

Joey began to pant, his breath coming in shallow gasps.

His eyes still shut, Joey slowly became aware that someone—or something—else was nearby. He knew this without seeing or hearing or smelling anything, almost as if he had developed a sixth sense, the way a snake can detect infrared heat, or a shark the weak electrical field given off by every living organism. Joey felt a shift in the displacement of air, the weight of a shadow falling on his skin.

"Stay away from me! Stay away from me!" he shrieked.

The odd, insistent sound of the wind chimes only got louder and faster.

. . . and at the hour of our deaths. Amen.

Before he could start the prayer a second time, Joey felt a touch on his arm. He flinched, then relaxed in surprise. The touch was as gentle as his mother's hand on his forehead when he had a fever. Startled, he opened his eyes for a second.

There was no one there.

Joey looked around in confusion. What was this place? It must be immense. The ceiling was so far away that it resembled a night sky, a thousand specks of light twinkling like strange constellations and a huge floodlamp glaring like the full moon.

The light reflected off something half-seen in the corner of Joey's eye, a shimmering, glistening shape that darted suddenly across his field of vision. Iridescent colors flashed, and for a moment Joey thought he glimpsed, not a face, but the three-dimensional outline of a face. It was like a transparent mask worn by an invisible man.

"Who's there?" Joey croaked.

The only answer was the tinkle of wind chimes.

Joey was panting so rapidly now that his breath seemed to start and end in his throat. Then he felt the touch again, on either side of his head.

"Who's there!" he shouted.

Joey tried to scramble to his feet, but he seemed to have no control over his arms and legs.

Something pushed him back down, gently but firmly, and the maddening sound of wind chimes repeated in his ear.

Joey felt a needle of cold inserted up one side of his nose. There was a sharp momentary pain, and he blacked out.

CHAPTER TWELVE

Monday, October 14, 4:05 P.M.

Dr. Kaminsky flashed a penlight in Joey's eyes. From somewhere in the emergency room a man began to cough, wheezing like a tired accordion.

Joey blinked and his hands flew to his nose, the stab of cold and pain still echoing along his nerves. He half expected to feel blood.

"It's all right, Joey," the doctor was saying. "You've had another seizure."

Joey sniffed. The trickle of fluid seeping into his nose felt too thin to be blood.

"Joey, can you hear me?"

He was tired, so tired that his jaw trembled with the effort of opening his mouth to speak. But he had to ask.

"The CAT scan," Joey whispered hoarsely, "the pictures you took of the inside of my head. Besides the fracture, did they show anything else wrong with me?"

Dr. Kaminsky raised his eyebrows. "Anything else?"

Joey looked down. This was going to be harder than he'd thought. He fixed his gaze on the doctor's purple tie. A cartoon moose and squirrel cavorted across it.

"I don't mean a tumor, you already told me it wasn't that, but . . ." He hesitated. "Did you see anything weird?

You know, like something missing or something that could never get there on its own?"

Dr. Kaminsky clicked off the penlight and tucked it in the pocket of his shirt. "What makes you ask that?"

Joey turned his head sideways, the paper runner that covered the examination table rustling beneath his ear. Gingerly he rubbed the side of his nose.

"Remember what I said about the unusual things you might experience before the start of a seizure?" Dr. Kaminsky said. "Funny smells, pictures in your head like scenes from a movie?"

Joey nodded.

"Doctors hear a lot of strange stories." Dr. Kaminsky smiled. "If you had some kind of vision, like a nightmare, I wish you'd tell me. I won't think you're crazy, Joey, I promise."

Joey stared at Rocky and Bullwinkle. "Did your son David give you that tie, too?"

Dr. Kaminsky glanced down. "No, I bought this for myself. I'm a big fan. I have the complete set of Rocky and Bullwinkle cartoons on videotape. But what makes you think there might be something weird in your CAT scan?"

Joey didn't answer. Dr. K might be cool enough to wear goofy ties, but that didn't mean he would believe that Joey's flashbacks were memories of something that really happened.

But Ethan Glass would. Joey had to get in touch with him right away.

A rivulet of fluid trickled onto Joey's upper lip. "Could

I please have a Kleenex?"

Dr. Kaminsky reached behind him and picked up a small box of tissues from the counter. "Do you remember anything, Joey?" he asked as he handed him the box.

Joey blew his nose. "Sorry, Dr. K. All I remember is riding the school bus with my brother Kevin, and the sunlight flashing in my eyes. Then I smelled burning wires again, and that was it."

Dr. Kaminsky sighed. "Okay."

Joey felt a twinge of guilt. He liked Dr. K.

The doctor scribbled a note on a clipboard and set it aside. "About your CAT scan," he said.

Joey took a deep breath. "Yeah?"

"I wanted to wait for your parents before we talked about this, but . . ." Dr. Kaminsky paused. "It did pick up an unusual shadow."

Joey jackknifed to a sitting position. "What kind of shadow?"

"I'm not sure. It appears to be a thin, oblong object of some sort, about an inch long, in the right temporal lobe of your brain."

"Where's that?"

"Here," Dr. Kaminsky said, touching the side of Joey's head, "between the ear and the nasal cavity."

The back of Joey's nose tingled, as if a tiny shock of static electricity had passed through it.

"I've got to see it." Joey's voice rose. "I've got to see those pictures."

"I'm sorry, Joey, I don't have them anymore. I sent

them to a specialist at the University of Virginia."

"A specialist? What kind of specialist? Why can't *you* take care of it?"

Dr. Kaminsky's mild blue eyes locked onto Joey's. "Whatever it is, the object may eventually have to be removed. I'm not a neurosurgeon; I'm not qualified to do that."

Joey shook his head vehemently. "Nobody's going to cut into my brain," he said.

Dr. Kaminsky bracketed Joey between his arms and leaned forward on the examination table. "I only said it *may* have to be removed. For now the doctor just wants your parents to bring you over to Charlottesville for another test, an MRI. It uses magnetic waves instead of x-rays to get a very detailed picture of your brain."

As if from far away, Joey heard the familiar melody of wind chimes singing in his ears. Gradually the sound changed, the endless tinkle of notes shifting, melting into bell-like syllables. It was like listening to a bird and pretending to hear words in its call.

"I don't want you to worry, Joey," Dr. K was saying. "This shadow we found, this object, doesn't appear to be threatening you in any way. The neurosurgeon didn't think it was urgent. He didn't schedule an appointment for you until the twenty-fifth.

The twenty-fifth of October, eleven days away. So he still had time.

"Until then, I'm going to prescribe some medication to stop these seizures you've been having."

Joey's ears rang again. The word "no" vibrated inside his head.

"I don't want any pills," he said.

There was too much he didn't remember yet, too much he didn't understand. He needed the seizures if he hoped to figure out what had happened to him up at the lake. As much as the seizures frightened him, he couldn't allow them to stop.

"Let's talk about this when your parents get here," Dr. Kaminsky said. "In the meantime, I'm afraid you're well enough to go back to school tomorrow." He shrugged and grinned. "Sorry I can't get you off the hook."

Joey grimaced. School. He'd almost forgotten he had to go back.

"I've got some other patients to check on," the doctor said. "I'll stop back when your parents arrive. You want a Coke or anything while you're waiting? My treat."

Joey nodded. "Sure." He suddenly realized his throat was parched.

Joey tipped his head back and drained the can of Coke. What was taking Mom and Dad so long to get to the hospital? He felt as if he'd been waiting here for ages.

But he knew it couldn't have been that long—he'd been so thirsty, he had finished his drink almost right away. Time seemed to like playing tricks on him lately: fast-forwarding him through two years of his life, then stranding him in guidance counselors' offices and sheriffs' cars and emergency rooms where the hands of the clock practically crawled around the dial.

Time. He hadn't wanted to believe Ethan Glass when he said time had stopped for Joey inside some alien spacecraft. It was a crackpot idea, too preposterous to take seriously.

But it fit, didn't it? Joey had been missing for two years, yet he hadn't aged a day. And how else could he explain what he had remembered during the seizures?

But there was something missing, something wrong. Not all the facts fit Ethan's theory. Where were the banks of computers you would expect to find in a spaceship, the expanse of gleaming metal, the clutter of instruments that looked like dental equipment? Joey had seen nothing like that during his flashback, just a huge floodlamp and a thousand lights scattered like stars across a distant dome.

And what about the aliens themselves? Joey remembered only one, and there was nothing monstrous about it, nothing slimy or scaly or clawed. Until that final, brief moment of pain, its touch had been gentle, and what Joey had seen of it through the fog of his fear was actually beautiful—the shimmer of colors flowing over the invisible form like mother-of-pearl.

Something chimed in his ear. *The door in the lake, the door in the lake—come back.*

Every muscle in Joey's body clenched. That voice again! Until today, he had heard it only at night, just before he fell asleep. Now he had heard it twice in broad daylight, while he was wide awake.

He glanced down at his hand. The Coke can was

crushed in his fist.

Stiffly, Joey opened his fingers and tossed the can in the trash. He probably shouldn't leave, but he had to find the restroom. He hopped down off the examination table and poked his head out into the corridor.

A young man in a short white lab coat pushed a cart along the gleaming linoleum floor. The cart rattled with racks of blood-filled test tubes, rubber stoppers colored red and purple and powder blue.

Joey forgot about finding a bathroom. Ariel worked part-time in the hospital lab. She could help him get in touch with Ethan, and together they would make sense of all this.

Crossing his fingers and praying she was on duty, Joey followed the young man down the hall. After turning several corners and taking the elevator down one floor, the young man finally wheeled his cart through a door that was marked HOSPITAL PERSONNEL ONLY. Joey's heart sank. Now how would he find out if Ariel was here? He stood rooted to the floor, staring blankly at the door and trying to think of a plan.

"Joey. What are you doing here?"

Joey smelled the faint scent of apples and whirled around. Ariel stood there in a white lab coat, her head cocked to one side.

"When you ran out of the dorm like that, well . . . I've been worried about you, Joey," Ariel said. "I know Ethan can get pretty intense, but he didn't mean to scare you."

"Where *is* Ethan?" Joey asked. "I sent him a message

on the computer Friday night, and he never answered."

"He was at a physics symposium down at Georgia Tech all weekend."

"I've got to talk to him," Joey said. "It's important. My memory is starting to come back."

Joey looked up at Ariel, and their eyes locked in understanding.

She consulted her watch. "He's got a late class now, but it's almost over. I could call him."

Joey's shoulders sagged. "That's no good. My parents are supposed to be upstairs right now talking to Dr. Kaminsky. And I can't come back over to the college. After I left last Friday without telling my mother, she called the sheriff on me."

"She called the sheriff?"

Joey lifted the corners of his mouth in an attempt at a smile. "She's still spooked about my disappearance. She won't let me out of her sight."

"So I guess your folks might be suspicious if two strange college kids showed up at your door, huh?" Ariel said. "We'll figure something out. Let me talk to Ethan, and we'll be in touch soon."

Joey nodded.

"Hang in there." Ariel patted his shoulder. "I've got to get back to work."

Joey raced back to the elevator, the thought that his parents might already be in the emergency room making him hurry.

A hand reached from behind him to press the elevator

button. "Going up?"

Joey turned in slow motion.

Kevin peered down at him quizzically. "Didn't you see me in the waiting room? I rode in the ambulance with you to the hospital. What are you doing way down here?"

"I was just looking for the men's room." Joey tried to laugh. "Guess I got a little lost."

"I'll say. You passed right by two of them." Kevin frowned. "Are you sure you're all right?"

"I'm fine. I didn't see them, that's all. These halls are pretty confusing." Joey grinned and did his best to look sheepish. He hoped it was convincing.

Kevin fixed with him a doubtful stare. "I don't know. It looked to me like you were following that lab guy. Then you met up with that girl. Who's she?"

"I don't know." Joey shrugged. "She was just giving me directions back to the ER."

"Right." Kevin crossed his arms over his chest. "Who are you trying to kid, Joey? I heard her call you by name. Where do you know her from?"

"It's none of your business, Kevin," Joey snapped. "Just never mind."

The elevator bell dinged and the doors slid open. The two brothers straddled the threshold, staring at each other.

"Tell me what's going on," Kevin demanded, stretching out his arm and blocking the entrance.

Joey's eyes clouded over. "I wish I knew, Kevin."

CHAPTER THIRTEEN

"Satisfactory, Mr. Finney. You may sit down."

Joey stood in front of Mr. Beatty's fifth-period history class, the sheet of looseleaf paper that held his outline for the oral report still trembling in his hands. A war that ended over two thousand years ago was the last thing he cared about. It wasn't ancient history that concerned him but *his* history, stitching together fragments of memory into something that made sense.

"Did you have another comment to make, Mr. Finney?" Mr. Beatty's words broke into Joey's thoughts.

The class tittered.

"No, sir." Joey shook his head. How long had he been standing there like an idiot? He scurried to his desk.

In the back of the classroom Dwayne Billue handed Carrie Beth Shelnutt two torn pieces of newsprint, stapled together at one corner. She covered her mouth and snorted like a pig.

"Ah, Miss Shelnutt," Mr. Beatty said, his back to the room as he wrote on the blackboard. "That laugh is unmistakable. Perhaps you could tell the class who fought the Punic Wars?"

Carrie Beth slouched in her chair and closed her eyes

101

so nothing but two smears of grape-colored eye shadow were visible. She twisted a strand of over-permed hair around her pencil. "I don't know. The Punes?"

The class erupted in laughter. Carrie Beth looked pleased with herself.

Brushing chalk from his hands, Mr. Beatty turned to face the room. The laughter died instantly. He acknowledged an arm waving in the front row. It belonged to Ganesh Patel, whose uncle owned the Minit Mart where Joey had been found.

"Yes, Mr. Patel?"

"The ancient Romans and Carthaginians fought the Punic Wars."

"Correct," Mr. Beatty said. He walked down the aisle toward Carrie Beth. "Now suppose you and Mr. Billue share that newspaper clipping you just passed. Something edifying, I trust."

"A lot better than a bunch of dead guys in chariots," someone murmured.

"Except maybe they aren't dead after all. Maybe the little green men beamed them up, too," another voice chimed in. A muted ripple of laughter spread through the room.

Joey stiffened. Was there something in the newspaper about aliens? Something about himself? But he had told only Ethan, and Ariel . . . and Hamp.

Mr. Beatty's voice cut through the laughter. "Does everyone wish to prepare an oral report for tomorrow? Now let me see the newspaper, please."

Carrie Beth handed it over. A few nervous giggles punctuated the silence as Mr. Beatty read the clipping. He glanced at Joey once, the expression in his eyes indecipherable. His face seemed to turn to stone.

Why was Mr. Beatty looking at him like that?

Come to think of it, a lot of the kids had been staring at him today. It was worse than yesterday. At least then it seemed they just didn't know what to say to him. But today they whispered and snickered in the hallways when he walked by, rolling their eyes and passing notes in class. Even the teachers had given him wary looks.

Mr. Beatty folded the clipping in half and walked to the classroom door. "Mr. Finney?"

Joey's mouth went dry. He eased out from his desk.

Mr. Beatty turned to face the class and tapped his watch. "There are still five minutes until the lunch bell. Turn to chapter seven in your textbooks and read. Silently. If I hear one word, everyone will be assigned a five-page report for tomorrow." Mr. Beatty beckoned Joey into the hall and pulled the door shut behind him, leaving it open a crack.

"Have you seen this, Joseph?" Mr. Beatty asked, his voice softer than in the classroom. Joey was startled. For the first time he realized that Mr. Beatty wasn't much taller than he was. Yet he seemed so big, so imposing, in class.

Joey scanned the piece of paper in his hand. It was from a column that the *Clarion* ran each week called "Sound Off." Readers called to complain or air their opinions, and the paper printed what they said; they didn't have to give their names. One segment was headlined LOCAL BOY CLAIMS ALIEN ABDUCTION.

Joey thought for a seemingly endless moment that his heart had stopped beating.

How did this get in the newspaper?

> The sheriff's not going to find Joey Finney's kidnapper from anyone on the FBI computer. At least not according to Joey. He says he was abducted by little green men from Mars or something. That's supposed to be how come he looks exactly the same as he did—because he was in some kind of time warp. This is really what he says. The guy needs help.

Joey closed his eyes. Hamp told.

Mr. Beatty spoke quietly. "What would you like to do now, Joseph?"

Mr. Beatty was offering him the chance to leave, to go to the office, to go home if he wanted to—anything to avoid having to face his classmates.

But the cafeteria was where Hamp would be. "I'll go on to lunch," Joey said.

Mr. Beatty nodded. "Very good," he said.

Joey blinked in surprise.

"I've never understood why the newspaper publishes this undocumented tripe," Mr. Beatty said, holding out his hand for the clipping. "Keep your head up, Joseph."

Joey walked back into class, proceeding straight to his desk and getting ready for the bell, aware that even if they weren't talking about him or looking at him, everyone was thinking about him and what the column in the *Clarion* had said.

But that didn't matter. All he cared about was getting to Hamp.

The bell rang and Joey rushed into the hall, shoving his way through the river of bodies flowing toward the cafeteria, oblivious to the stares and whispers.

He marched into the lunchroom. Kevin ran up to him with a copy of the *Clarion* and tapped him on the arm with it.

"Is this true? Did you actually tell something like this to Hamp?"

"I know, I know, you warned me," Joey said impatiently. "Not now, Kevin."

Kevin stepped in front of him and blocked his path. "Is this what you were talking about to that girl at the hospital?"

Joey said nothing and bumped Kevin aside. He strode up to the table where Brett and Amy and Hamp were sitting. Joey could feel the blood pounding in his head.

"I asked you to keep it secret," Joey said, "and you told."

Hamp didn't even glance up. He pried the lid off a plastic bottle of apple juice.

"Yeah, so what?" said Brett, kicking back his chair and leaning over the table. "Hamp can do what he wants. He doesn't need to ask your permission."

"I'm not talking to you," Joey said, ice in his voice.

"Sit down, Brett." Hamp inspected the turkey and ham sandwich the Durdens' housekeeper had made for him, and removed a slice of tomato.

"Does he do everything you tell him to?" Joey asked. "Including calling the paper? Or did you do that yourself?"

"What difference does it make?" Hamp said. He took a bite of his sandwich.

Joey slammed his hands down on the table, rattling the silverware in Brett's and Amy's lunch trays. "It makes a difference to me!" he shouted. "You shouldn't have told, Hamp. You promised."

A hush began to settle over the normally noisy cafeteria.

Hamp put down his sandwich and swallowed what he had in his mouth. He grimaced slightly, as if the food hurt his throat. "I never promised," he said. "You asked me if I could keep a secret, but I never promised you anything."

Joey pushed away from the table and straightened up. "Used to be just asking you would have been enough."

"Yeah, well, things were different then. I was different." Hamp met Joey's eyes for a second, then looked away. "Don't you get it, Joey? The way you are now, you just don't fit in."

The lunchroom was completely silent, but noise thundered in Joey's ears—the sound not of an alien voice, but of his own anger and loss and betrayal. He picked up the bottle of apple juice and dumped it in Hamp's lap.

Hamp jumped up, knocking his chair over backwards.

Ms. D'Amato came running over, blowing her nose like a trumpet into a handful of Kleenex. "All right, boys. What's going on here?"

Brett opened his mouth and was about to speak when Hamp clamped one hand on his shoulder. "I just spilled my juice." A large, dark stain was spreading rapidly across the crotch of his chinos.

Ms. D'Amato sneezed. "I've got a miserable cold, Hampton. Don't try to con me today. The entire lunchroom could hear you two."

"I told you, I spilled my juice." Pinching his thumbs and forefingers together, Hamp pulled the wet fabric of his pants away from his legs. "Could I go to the office and call home for some clean clothes?"

Ms. D'Amato glared at Hamp but allowed him to leave. "You," she said to Joey, "get some lunch and sit at the teachers' table where I can keep an eye on you."

"I'm not hungry."

She honked into her Kleenex again. "Get your lunch and go sit."

Joey went through the line and paid for a tray of food that he had no intention of eating. That stupid article. Kids must have been passing it around all morning, and like an idiot he never realized it. Suddenly he stopped dissecting his food, dropping his knife and fork into the gluey sauce. Everybody in Cornish Gap read the *Clarion*.

Mom and Dad—they would read the article. So would Dr. Kaminsky. And the sheriff, too.

Wind chimes began to sound in his ears, and Joey

braced himself for the words he knew were coming.

The door in the lake, the door in the lake—come.

Joey shoved his tray aside. Maybe he should listen. Anything would be better than what was waiting for him at home.

CHAPTER FOURTEEN

The late afternoon sun slanted through the living room window, casting four skewed squares of amber light on the carpet. Joey sat in a wing chair by the fireplace, facing the three people on the couch: Mom, Dad, and Sheriff Varnadoe, balancing a cup and saucer on his broad knees. A copy of the *Clarion* lay unfolded on the coffee table.

"Well?" his father demanded.

Joey wished for a glass of water, or better yet, a mug of his mother's standard cold remedy—hot tea mixed with a spoonful of powdered lemonade. His throat was dry and scratchy.

"Aliens from outer space." His father picked up the newspaper by its edges, as if it were soiled, then tossed it back down on the table. "Whoever called in will just have to print an apology. I'm sure you never said any such thing. Did you?"

Joey was silent.

Sheriff Varnadoe eyed him over the rim of his coffee cup. He took a swallow, then set the cup back down in the saucer with a clatter that sounded loud in the stillness of the living room.

Joey's mother rubbed one temple. "You lived through

a nightmare these past two years, honey. You were snatched away from us in the middle of the night . . . " Her voice faltered. "I can understand your not wanting to face the truth just yet, but making up a story like this doesn't help."

"Making it up?" his father said. "Did you actually tell someone this nonsense about aliens? Answer me, Joey."

Mrs. Finney turned to her husband. "Dan," she said, folding her hand over his and gripping it tightly.

She turned back to look at Joey. "Sometimes it's too painful to remember the real things that have happened to you. Maybe it's easier to believe that some creature from a movie or one of your science fiction books took you away."

Easier to believe? What a laugh. It wasn't easy at all. But there was no point in saying anything.

The phone shrilled from the computer table against the far wall. His father got up to answer it.

"Who?" he said sharply. "No, absolutely not. My son is not giving any interviews." He slammed down the phone.

Joey's mother twisted around on the couch. "Who was that?"

"You're not going to believe this," Joey's father said, "but it was a reporter for the Roanoke paper. They wanted to do a story on Joey." He groaned. "This is becoming a circus. Maybe you were right, Beth—maybe we should have gone away."

Sheriff Varnadoe hoisted himself off the couch, walked over to the fireplace, and leaned against the mantel. "Joey still hasn't answered the question."

Joey swallowed, and wished again for some water or tea. His spit hurt going down.

"Is the newspaper story accurate, son? Did you tell a friend that you were abducted by aliens?"

Joey remained silent.

His parents looked at him intently.

"Is that what you believe?" the sheriff asked.

Joey studied the bulletin board that hung on the wall behind the computer. His own face smiled back at him from the flyers tacked to the cork.

Who was that boy, Joey wondered. What did he have to smile about? Had he just caught a pop fly that ended the ninth inning and won the game for his team? Had he finally saved up enough allowance to buy that new video game he had his heart set on?

Was he about to go on a camping trip with his family and best friend?

Joey stared at the face on the bulletin board. It was the same face he saw in the mirror each morning, but he didn't know who it was anymore. The boy grinning down from the wall was a stranger to him now.

"Joey, answer the sheriff," his father said. "That isn't what you believe, is it?"

Joey took a deep breath. "Yes, it is."

His mother covered her eyes with one hand. "I should have listened to Ms. D'Amato. I should have taken you to a therapist."

"You don't expect us to believe such rubbish." His

father's voice was cold, the grooves around his mouth deep and sharp.

Sheriff Varnadoe rested his arm against the back of the wing chair, and Joey could hear the leather in his belt and holster creaking. "Don't be so hard on the boy, Dan. I'll tell you this—Joey sincerely believes he is speaking the truth."

Joey stared fixedly at the four sunlit squares on the carpet. Without looking, he could still feel the weight of his father's gaze on him.

"Of course, that doesn't mean it *is* the truth," the sheriff went on. "I think we know better than that. But don't fault the boy for lying."

"I don't want to argue with you, Wade," Joey's father said, "but if it isn't true, then he must be lying. And he is going to get on that phone right now and tell the newspaper so."

Joey stared down at his lap and began to shake his head. "I can't, Dad."

"What did I just hear you say?"

Joey slowly lifted his head to look his father full in the face. He had never defied him before. "I can't."

His father half rose off the couch. "Don't tell me no."

"Stop it." His mother tugged at his sleeve, and Joey's father reluctantly sat back down. "Calling the paper isn't going to solve anything. I almost wish Joey were lying, but his problem isn't that simple."

"You think I'm crazy," Joey said, glancing at his mother. A pained smile froze on her lips. "You do too, don't you,

112

Sheriff?"

The phone jangled, startling everyone.

"Let me handle this one," Sheriff Varnadoe offered. He picked up the receiver and listened, his face changing. "I'll have to check on that. Beth, Dan—it's one of Joey's young friends from school. Is it all right if he takes it?"

Joey frowned. What friends did he have at school?

His mother's face darkened. "I'm not sure. Who is it?"

The sheriff was opening his mouth to ask when the front doorbell rang in three short bursts.

"What now?" his father growled, lunging off the couch.

Joey's mother went to the window and peeked around the curtain. "Oh, no."

"More reporters?" The sheriff rested the phone on his shoulder.

Joey's father glanced outside through the window. "Looks like a television news crew. Can you believe it, Channel 12 coming all the way up from Richmond for this?"

"I suggest we talk to them together—outside, on the porch," Sheriff Varnadoe said. "Joey, you stay here, and keep well back from the window."

The sheriff escorted Mr. and Mrs. Finney into the hall, and Joey heard a brief gabble of noisy, insistent voices as the front door open and shut.

He dragged himself over to the computer table and put the forgotten phone to his ear, holding it out from his head as if it might bite him. Probably Hamp or Brett or one of their joker friends trying to razz him some more. Maybe they had gotten tired of waiting and hung up by now.

"Finney?" The muscles in Joey's body unclenched when he heard the voice.

"Ethan." Joey's breath came out in a rush. "I didn't expect to hear from you."

"Yeah, well, I read the *Clarion* this morning. Who was that who answered the phone?"

"The sheriff."

"Ouch," Ethan said. "Is it safe to talk?"

Glancing over his shoulder to make sure his parents and the sheriff hadn't come back inside, Joey turned his back to the hall archway and faced the wall. "Everybody's on the front porch with a bunch of reporters from TV."

"Man, you really stepped in it."

"Did you call to tell me that?"

"No. Ari told me your memory was starting to come back." Ethan sounded excited.

"What I'm remembering doesn't make a lot of sense," Joey said. "I really need to talk to you guys, privately."

"Name the time and place."

Joey hesitated. There was no way Ethan and Ariel could just show up at his front door: how would he explain them to his parents? "My folks usually go to bed pretty early," he said. "I'll try to sneak out after they're asleep, say about midnight? You could meet me where the street dead-ends in the woods."

Ethan agreed, and in the silence after he said goodbye Joey heard a faint crackling. It took him a moment to realize it was the phone line and not the static in his head. There was no ringing in his ears, no choppy words summoning him to the lake.

It didn't matter. He had heard enough already today—from his parents, the sheriff, and his so-called friends. He didn't need another voice to tell him what to do. Joey stared at the boy smiling down from the bulletin board and wished there were some way he could trade places with him, some way he could get back to the way he used to be.

CHAPTER FIFTEEN

Tuesday, October 15, 11:22 P.M.

"Are you okay, honey?" his mother asked, sitting on the edge of Joey's bed.

"I'm fine, Mom."

Even the gentle glow of lamplight could not disguise the tracery of worry lines etched around her eyes. Joey felt a hollowness at the base of his throat: he had given her these lines. He had probably added a few more this afternoon.

"Did you take your medication?" she asked.

"Uh-huh." Joey swallowed the words as soon as he said them. Lying. He was going to have to admit that to Father Kinsella in confession this week. He hadn't been taking the pills Dr. Kaminsky prescribed to stop his seizures; he had flushed them down the toilet instead.

"Try to get some sleep," his mother said, smoothing his hair off his forehead. "It's late."

She kissed his cheek and left, closing the door softly behind her.

Joey jiggled his feet under the blankets and stared at the digital clock glowing beside him in the darkness: 11:22. His excursion to the hospital had set back the entire family's schedule. They were all late getting to bed, even

Molly. But there was no way to get word to Ethan and Ariel. He just hoped everyone would be asleep by midnight so he could safely steal outside.

The neon red numbers on the bedside clock blinked off the minutes: 11:34, 11:35. Gradually a stillness settled over the house. It was not completely silent; Joey could hear occasional groans as boards contracted, releasing heat built up over the day, and water gurgling in the pipes and the old steam radiators.

The minutes dragged, crawling by so slowly that Joey swore time had come to a halt. He half expected the numbers on his clock to stop, then start counting in reverse.

If only time could move backward, he thought. If only he could somehow recover the two years he had lost.

Finally the clock read 11:53. Joey threw off the blankets and grabbed a flashlight from the drawer of his bedside table. The hinges squealed as he pulled open the bedroom door, seeming to make an awful racket. He froze, but no one came out. He crept into the hall.

He was just outside Kevin's door when he stumbled up against something large and furry and went sprawling against the banister. Joey swore under his breath, another offense for confession.

"Magnum!" he whispered. The big dog, his black coat a perfect camouflage in the darkness, thumped his tail against the floor. "Shh! Don't make so much noise."

Joey crouched down and hunched over the dog, stroking his back to keep him quiet. He waited several seconds, but still no one stirred.

"Stay," he commanded, then tiptoed down the staircase. Magnum immediately got up and tagged along behind, trailing Joey into the kitchen and out onto the back porch.

Joey blew out a sigh, his breath forming clouds in the crisp October night, as he closed the screen door carefully behind him.

He looked up. The stars glittered like chips of ice in the obsidian sky. The Great Square of Pegasus rode the peak of Burnt Mountain, and in the east the familiar H-shaped constellation of Orion stood astride a waning moon. Thousands of specks of light crowded the dome of the sky.

Just like the place he remembered in his seizures.

Joey hugged himself and tried to rub away the goose bumps rising on his arms. He was tired of being afraid. He felt a restless urge to do something. Anything.

He switched on his flashlight and hurried down the street, scuffing through the sea of leaves that covered the sidewalk. He crossed under the half-naked branches of a big maple and turned into the woods. A light flashed in his eyes, and his heart began to hammer in his chest. Beside him Magnum issued a low, throaty growl.

"Finney? Is that you?"

His heart slowed its hammering. "Ethan?"

"Your dog doesn't bite, does he?"

"No. Not friends." Joey ran his hand under the dog's chin. "It's okay, Magnum."

"Come here, boy." Joey recognized Ariel's voice. Magnum promptly abandoned him and trundled over to the girl, his tail wagging.

Ariel laughed. "Some watchdog. What kind is he, Joey?"

"A Newfoundland."

"Did we come out here to talk about dogs?" Ethan asked. "Douse the lights." The brightness that was blinding Joey winked off. "We don't want the neighbors getting suspicious and calling the police."

Joey switched off his own flashlight, and his eyes slowly adjusted to the darkness. All he could see of Ethan was the moonlight reflecting off the lenses of his glasses.

"Tell me." Ethan's voice was filled with eagerness. "What do you remember?"

But now that he at last had someone he could tell, Joey found it difficult to get the words out. There was a long silence before he finally said, "There was some kind of alien."

"I knew it," Ethan exulted. "What did it look like?"

"I don't know."

"What do you mean, you don't know?"

"Ethan," Ariel warned. "What did I tell you about getting so intense?"

"Sorry." He sounded genuinely contrite. "I'm just . . . This is just so amazing."

"You don't remember what it looked like, Joey?" Ariel asked.

"I never got a good look at it," he said. "It was like I could only see it out of the corner of my eye. And when I did try to look straight at it, all I caught was this flash of color—like the reflection of a rainbow in a puddle of water."

Ethan reached up and snapped a branch off the tree. "What about the spacecraft then, what did it look like? How did they get you inside?"

"I didn't really see it either," Joey said, dragging out the words, fearing that he was a big disappointment to Ethan. "I think it came out of the lake."

"Out of the lake?" Ethan echoed.

"Yeah. When I came out of the . . . the l-latrine"—Joey stumbled over the word, conscious that Ariel was listening—"that's when I noticed that the whole lake was glowing."

"Glowing." Ethan repeated Joey again.

"Then this huge thing rose out of the lake, high above my head, spinning like some kind of inside-out tornado. And I was just sort of lifted up through the air."

Remembering it, Joey trembled. Ariel moved closer and squeezed his shoulder.

"I was pushed or sucked through something. I could feel it but I couldn't see it."

"A force field," Ethan said. "Then what?"

"I was inside, I guess. It was gigantic. I didn't see any walls or a ceiling, just a lot of lights that seemed pretty far away."

"No computers or instrument panels?"

"Nothing like that." Half to himself, Joey added, "Actually, it was more like being outside than inside."

Ethan shook his head. "This doesn't sound much like

other abduction reports."

"You're the expert on this stuff," Joey said. "What does it mean?"

Ethan was silent. Then, "Look, Joey, I never said I was an expert."

Joey's ears began to roar. "Is this all a big joke?" he asked, choking out the words as he had choked on those peppercorns when he was eight. "See if you can put one over on the stupid little junior high schooler?"

"No."

Ariel cleared her throat. "Tell him, Ethan."

Joey looked back and forth between them, squinting to see their faces in the silvery moonlight.

"When Ari overheard those nurses talking about you at the hospital, I had to get in touch with you . . . " Ethan's voice trailed off.

Joey waited as the silence stretched out.

"I saw something once," Ethan said at last, his voice so low that Joey had to strain to hear it. "When I was ten. Just a glimpse, a funny green star that zigzagged all over the sky one winter night. I've been looking for it ever since, trying to find out if it was real."

Joey's hopes leaked out of him like air from an old balloon. "A funny green star, is that all you saw? You don't know any more than I do." Fluid trickled out of his nose. He swiped at it with the back of his hand. "If you can't help me, who can?"

"We can help you, Joey," Ariel said.

"How?" Joey turned away. "You can't fix what's wrong.

I'm nothing but a joke to my friends. I don't fit in with my own family. And I'm walking around with some thing in my head that Dr. K says may need to be cut out."

"Whoa, what are you talking about?" Ethan asked. "What haven't you told us?"

Joey let out a shuddering sigh. "The alien put something up my nose. Now spinal fluid leaks out all the time, and the CAT scan shows an odd shadow in part of my brain . . . and it's not a tumor."

"It's a tracking device," Ethan said.

"It's a basilar skull fracture," Ariel countered. "You can't know for sure what caused it."

"I've read about this," Ethan persisted. "The aliens supposedly use them to mark people, the way we band birds and wildlife."

"Why would they want to do that?" Joey asked, his voice rising.

"Sit down," Ethan said, walking over and putting his hand on Joey's arm.

"Why?"

"They come back, Joey," Ethan said. "From what I've read, the aliens often come back and take the same people, over and over again."

The marrow of Joey's bones grew cold.

"Ethan!" Ariel said sharply. "You've got no business telling him that."

"He's right." Joey's voice was dull.

"No, Joey, he's just guessing."

"It *is* coming back," Joey said.

"What makes you so sure?" Ethan asked.

"It talks to me," Joey said. "There's this ringing in my ears all the time, and sometimes it starts to sound like wind chimes, and then I can hear it talking inside my head. It keeps telling me to come to the lake, come to the door in the lake."

Above them, a tree branch creaked in a sudden downdraft of air. They all jumped.

"What can I do?" Joey pleaded.

Ariel corrected him. "What can *we* do," she said.

Joey felt a surge of gladness, and the ice in his bones melted a little.

"First, we need to get more information," Ethan said. "We don't have enough to go on yet. If only you remembered more."

"Every time I have a seizure, I get another piece of my memory back," Joey said. "Dr. Kaminsky prescribed some pills to stop the seizures, but I'm not taking them. Maybe we could trigger one somehow, on purpose."

"Absolutely not!" said Ariel. "It's not safe."

"There's hypnosis," Ethan suggested. "That's the way most abduction victims recall what happened to them."

"Do either of you know how to do that?" Joey asked.

"No," Ariel said. "And I don't think any professional would hypnotize you without your parents' permission either."

Ethan sighed and twisted his ponytail with one hand. "Well then, the only thing I can think of is to go back through all the newspaper reports and computer files we can find that link Smokewater Lake with similar abduction experiences."

"No," Joey said.

Ariel and Ethan turned to look at him, their faces pale in the moonlight.

"We can go up there."

Neither of them said a word.

Joey punched his fist into his palm. Maybe there was a way to fix everything. Time is elastic, isn't that what Ethan said? If the alien who had stolen Joey was able to manipulate time to make it go forward, then it might be able to reverse it too. It might somehow be able to bring him back to the night he left, before he ever unzipped his sleeping bag to go to the lake. Maybe.

And if not, there was nowhere he could hide anyway. He lifted his chin in the air. "I'm not just going to sit around and be afraid anymore. You want to know if it's real, don't you?"

Ethan's only answer was the gleam of his glasses.

"No," Ariel said. "It's too dangerous. Going back up to Smokewater Lake is the last thing we should do."

CHAPTER SIXTEEN

Wednesday, October 16, 6:30 A.M.

Joey slept fitfully, darting just under the surface of sleep like a fish swimming in a shallow pond. His dreams were filled with strobelike images: kaleidoscopes of light and color arcing through the sky, treetops slapping against his ankles, and the elusive ghost of a face—glistening, prismatic—that he could never quite make out.

He awoke in a sweat. He had to return to Smokewater Lake, he had to end this. If Ariel and Ethan wouldn't help him, he'd find some other way to get there. But how? All he had was a bike, and it was almost forty miles up winding mountain roads to the lake.

His throat was on fire and a dull headache thudded behind the bridge of his nose. He remembered Ms. D'Amato honking and sneezing yesterday. Great. As if she hadn't done enough for him already, now she had given Joey her cold.

Joey felt the draining sensation in his nose again, but it was different this morning. Slower, thicker, like a nosebleed that has finally begun to clot. He grabbed a tissue from the box on his bedside table and blew, a needle of pain jabbing into his skull. Gone was the clear, straw-colored cerebrospinal fluid. The tissue was stained with green, blood-streaked pus.

A cold. It was just a bad cold. If he let Mom see that he was sick, she'd panic and drag him to the hospital again to see Dr. K, and then he'd never be able to steal away and get to the lake. He couldn't let anything stop him.

Joey dragged himself out of bed and to the bathroom. He leaned over the sink to rinse out his mouth, drinking straight from the faucet. Ow! It hurt to bend his neck. He must have slept on it funny.

Joey plodded back to his room and got dressed, shivering and sinking down on the bed to rest after he put on each item of clothing: jeans, turtleneck, sweatshirt, and flannel shirt. Magnum wandered in and poked him with a damp nose.

Joey lay his head stiffly on the mattress, to avoid jarring his sore neck, and pulled the dog's giant head down beside him. "I wish you could come with me today, Mags."

The dog scooted closer, inching the front half of his body onto the bed and thumping his tail against the double row of drawers beneath it.

"But it's not safe."

Magnum's tail grew still.

"Who knows what's up at the lake? And I don't want you to end up like me. I wouldn't wish my life on anybody, not even Brett or Hamp."

Joey rolled off the bed and rose to his feet, swaying a little as he waited for the spots before his eyes to clear. This cold was a whopper.

He plugged his ears with his fingers and strained to hear through the ever-present static, listening for any last words from the voice inside his head.

Nothing. He was on his own.

Luck was with him. Mom had left early for work. If she had seen his flushed cheeks and his glassy eyes, he would never have been able to convince her that he was just tired. But it was easy to fool Dad, his hands full getting Molly dressed and fed, his face still tight with anger over Joey's refusal to relent and say he had made up the whole alien-abduction story.

Kevin eyed him curiously, however. "You don't look so hot, Joey. You coming down with something?"

"Nope." Joey zipped up his jacket.

"Jeez, Joey, it's not that cold out."

"I'm freezing."

Kevin shook his head. "If I were you, I'd use any excuse to get out of going to school today. And here you are passing up a perfectly good case of the flu. I don't get it."

Joey slung his backpack over his shoulder. "And end up with Mrs. Nuttall force-feeding me ginger ale and saltines all day? Butt out, Kevin. I'm all right."

Kevin peered at Joey through narrowed eyes. "Have it your way," he said, banging open the front door. He headed down the sidewalk toward the bus stop, looking back over his shoulder toward the house.

Joey was amazed at how easy it was to slip away from school. He waited until Kevin got off the bus and disappeared into the front lobby, then got off himself. He edged his way through the mob of kids being disgorged from cars and other buses and simply walked off. Nobody noticed him; nobody tried to stop him. No wonder kids cut class.

He walked about a mile down the road, trying to ignore the headache that was throbbing behind his eyes now, making them feel as if they were bulging out of his face.

When he got to Hwy. 220, he thought it was safe to stick out his thumb and flag down a ride.

Nobody stopped. Joey resumed walking, stripping off first his jacket, then his flannel shirt as he grew hotter and hotter. His legs began to feel rubbery and weak. He would never make it to the lake on foot.

God, he begged, please make somebody stop.

Ten minutes later a big semi rig downshifted and pulled over on the shoulder a hundred yards down the highway. Afraid that the driver wouldn't wait, Joey hobbled to the truck as fast as he could manage. He could rest on the way up to the lake. But at least now he would get there. He breathed a prayer of thanks.

It took all his strength to pull himself up into the cab. He was greeted by a burly man with a dark growth of stubble on his face and chin. Vince Gill blared from the radio.

"Where you headed, boy?" the man asked. "Ain't it a school day?"

Joey was ready for this. "It's a teacher work day. You

know, they have conferences and catch up with paper-work and stuff. So we get the day off." He was ashamed at how glibly the lie rolled off his tongue.

"That so?" the driver said, picking up a styrofoam cup with the words MINIT MART printed on it and draining it in one gulp. He kept his eyes on Joey while he drank.

Joey squirmed a little in his seat. To avoid the driver's eyes, he looked around the cab. A six-pack of pecan twirls sat on the dash, all but two of them eaten. Down inside a plastic trash bag hanging from one of the knobs on the radio Joey could see the cellophane wrappers of several other packs.

"Your folks know you thumb rides?"

Joey tensed and twisted sideways on the seat, ready to jump out. Had this guy picked him up just to give him a lecture?

The driver leaned across Joey and slammed the truck door shut.

"Go on, buckle up tight now. I didn't say I wouldn't give you a lift." The driver shifted into first, checked his mirrors, and edged back onto the highway.

As he twisted around to pull down the seat belt from a hook near the ceiling of the cab, a small groan escaped Joey. Pain gripped his neck.

The driver shot him a look but didn't comment. "How far you going?"

"Jefferson National Forest," Joey said, staring out the windshield at the hunchbacked mountains rising before them. He wished the driver would stop talking. Answering his questions took too much energy, and he didn't have any to spare. He would need all his strength once he got to the lake.

"Kinda late in the year for camping, isn't it?"

Joey sighed. "I . . . I'm meeting someone up there. Just for the day." It wasn't a total lie. He was going to the lake to meet someone.

Joey shivered as a wave of chills swept through him. He had been hot just a minute ago. Struggling with the seat belt, he managed to get his flannel shirt back on but had to settle for draping the jacket around his shoulders.

The truck driver stole another look at him. Why did he keep doing that, Joey wondered. It was making him nervous.

"You look kinda familiar," the driver said. He scratched the stubble on his chin. "My name's Levon. Don't I know you from someplace?"

Joey licked his lips. "No." He began to get the feeling that the trucker wasn't going to take him to the lake after all.

"I'm sure I seen your face somewhere," Levon persisted. He stepped on the brakes. "And you weren't looking too good then neither. I guess that's why you don't remember me."

"I don't know you," Joey said, sliding farther away from the driver. He just wanted to get out of the truck and find another ride to the lake. "Why don't you let me out here?"

The truck jolted over a pothole in the road, and a bolt

of pain rocketed down Joey's neck. He moaned.

Levon tugged the big steering wheel around to the left. "Well, I sure know you, Joseph Patrick Finney. You're the lost boy," he said. "And you ain't going camping today. I'm taking you to the hospital."

Dr. Kaminsky crouched down so his eyes were on a level with Joey's. "I'm afraid we're going to have to do another spinal tap."

Joey tried to nod, but the slightest movement of his head was excruciating. Even lying flat on the gurney, his headache had grown so severe that it seemed he could feel every corpuscle of blood pounding painfully through the veins in his head.

Dr. Kaminsky stood up. "I like your tie," Joey whispered, staring at a field of grinning orange jack-o-lanterns on a black background.

"Halloween's just two weeks away," Dr. Kaminsky said. "I steered clear of skeletons and ghosts and vampires—not the best advertisement for a hospital. I thought it might scare patients into thinking they'd come to the wrong place."

Joey managed a weak smile. "You don't scare me, Dr. K."

"What a brave guy." The doctor placed his hands gently on Joey's shoulders. "I need you to be brave a few minutes longer. I've got to get that lumbar puncture now. Ready?"

The doctor rolled Joey over on his side, and every

nerve in his head and neck fired in agony. As Dr. Kaminsky punctured his spine with the needle and withdrew some fluid, Joey gripped the rails on the side of the gurney so tight that his knuckles showed white through the skin.

"I'm going to send this down to the lab for tests, but I already have a pretty good idea what's wrong with you, Joey."

"Can I get out of here soon, then?"

"You're not going anywhere," Dr. Kaminsky said, carefully lowering Joey flat on his back and covering him with a blanket. "You've got meningitis. Do you know what that is?"

Joey was silent.

"It's an infection of the lining that covers your brain and spinal cord. The fracture in your sinus left an open door for bacteria to get from your nose into your brain." Dr. Kaminsky paused. "You're one sick boy."

Joey braced himself, then blinked. Even that slight movement hurt. "Sounds bad. So give me some pills and send me home."

"What's the big hurry?" Dr. Kaminsky pulled up a wheeled stool and sat down. "The truck driver you hitched a ride with said you were heading up to the national forest. What do you think is up there, Joey?"

Joey stared at the pumpkins on the doctor's tie. "You read the paper yesterday, didn't you?"

Dr. Kaminsky nodded. "So that's what you were holding back from me about your seizures. I knew there was something."

"Because you wouldn't have believed me," Joey said, lifting his head with great strain. "It isn't just tricks my mind is playing on me, Dr. K. Do you think I want to believe that stuff really happened to me? But it did—I remember it."

Joey collapsed back against the gurney. Every nerve in his head was screaming, but what hurt even more was the knowledge that now even Dr. K would think he was a nut case.

"Okay," Dr. K said, rolling back the stool and standing up. "Then there should be evidence to prove it."

Joey looked up in surprise. "You don't think I'm crazy."

Dr. Kaminsky smiled. "I told you once I'd always take you seriously." He picked up an otoscope and peered through the lens. "Doctors are like detectives—always searching for clues. What have you got?"

"Well," Joey began, "how could I be gone two years and not get any older?"

"Joey, you're fourteen now."

"Do I look fourteen to you?" Joey asked.

Now it was Dr. Kaminsky's turn to say nothing.

"And what about the CAT scan? That thing in my head? How could it get in there and leave nothing but a—what did you call it—a hairline fracture?"

Dr. Kaminsky's forehead creased. "I don't know what the answer is, Joey. But what you're claiming . . . " He broke off as a nurse swept back the curtain and entered the examination room with an IV cart.

"We'll talk later, Joey. Right now it's urgent that we get some antibiotics into your bloodstream. The nurse is going to start an IV, and we're going to do some more tests—blood work, x-rays. Then we'll move you upstairs to intensive care."

Joey frowned. "Intensive care? How bad is meningitis?"

Dr. Kaminsky covered Joey's hand with his own. "It's nothing to fool around with, Joey."

"Does anybody ever die from it?" A chill that had nothing to do with Joey's fever swept over his body.

Dr. Kaminsky's eyes were steady behind his wire rims. "We're not going to let that happen."

Joey closed his eyes. He could die.

"We'll find an orderly to get you down to radiology," Dr. Kaminsky said. "I've got to get hold of your parents. Then I'll be back." He and the nurse left the room.

Noise began to roar in his ears, louder and louder. Crackling in the background so he could barely make them out were the words: *The door in the lake, the door in the lake. Come now, come NOW, co —*

And then the words broke up, dissolving back into the static like a weak signal on a radio dial.

He had to get to the lake. With an effort that left sweat running down his face, Joey pushed himself upright, ripped out his IV, and swung his legs over the edge of the gurney.

The room darkened before his eyes, the pain in his head so intense that it felt as if his skull would surely explode. He heard the clink of metal rings as the curtain was pulled back, and with a sinking heart he realized that someone had caught him. He wasn't going to make it out of the hospital after all. The orderly was here.

He smelled a faint scent of apples, and heard a familiar voice.

"Where do you think you're going, Finney?"

Ariel and Ethan.

Joey blacked out.

CHAPTER SEVENTEEN

Wednesday, October 16, 9:55 A.M.

Groping his way back to consciousness through a blind haze of fever and pain, Joey recognized a male voice.

"We've got to get him out of here."

Cool fingers brushed against his forehead. "And take him where? To the lake? So you can test some pet theory about little green men from Mars? I'm not going to let you do it, Ethan."

"Pet theory?" There was a sharp intake of breath. "Thanks a lot, Ari. I thought you at least had an open mind."

Joey's lids fluttered and he opened his eyes. Ariel and Ethan stood over him, facing each other across the gurney like boxers in the ring. Ariel reached over and laid her hand on Ethan's arm.

"You're the one who's closed your mind," she said. "All you seem to care about is proving that what you saw when you were a kid was real."

Ethan jerked away from her grasp.

Ariel glared at him. "This has become an obsession. When you're prepared to sacrifice Joey . . . "

"You just don't get it, do you?" Ethan said. "If we don't take him to the lake, you and your precious doctors will be the ones hurting him."

Joey inched his fingers upward and tugged on the sleeve of Ariel's lab coat. "He's right," he said hoarsely.

Both Ariel and Ethan looked down in surprise.

"I've got to get to the lake. Now."

Ariel marched over to the examining room curtain. "The only thing you've got to do is get a new IV running. I'll find a nurse, and then we'll get you down to radiology."

"No!" The word echoed in spasms of pain throughout Joey's skull.

Ariel paused.

Joey steeled himself and grabbed the rails, but he wasn't strong enough to sit. He looked at Ethan. "Please," he whispered, and Ethan hooked his hands under Joey's arms and lifted him up.

Joey leaned back against Ethan and waited for the drumbeat of pain in his head to subside. "Ethan's right. I have to get to the lake."

Ariel walked back to the gurney. "Meningitis is no joke, Joey. Without treatment the infection will spread. First you'll have convulsions, then you'll go into a coma. And when that happens there is no guarantee that even the strongest drugs will bring you out of it—ever."

"I know how sick I am," Joey said in a low voice.

Exasperated, Ariel threw her hands in the air.

"Listen to me, Ari," Ethan said. "I've been thinking. What if I was wrong the other night when I said that the object in Joey's head was a tracking device?"

Ariel's eyes flashed. "So now you're admitting that you might be wrong? I suppose that's progress."

Ethan scowled. "Come off it, Ari. What if it's some kind of transponder, a device the alien is using to talk to Joey? That would explain—"

"The voice in my head," Joey broke in.

Ethan and Ariel said nothing.

"It's been calling me," Joey said, "telling me to come to the door in the lake, whatever that is. But it stopped a while ago." He pressed his fingers against one ear. "Just broke off in the middle of a word. I don't think that's a good sign."

Ethan locked glances with Ariel. "See?" he said to her.

"I see, all right." The pink curtain partitioning off the examination room was yanked aside, and Kevin stepped in.

The last frail spark of hope in Joey's heart flickered and died. That was it. Ethan might eventually have convinced Ariel about the need to get to Smokewater Lake, but nothing would sway Kevin. Joey closed his eyes and slid flat on his back.

Ethan leaned down and whispered into Joey's ear. "Who is this guy?"

"My brother," Joey said. "He's going to be a problem."

Ethan pulled himself to his full height. "How long have you been hanging around out there?"

"Long enough." Kevin walked over and stood next to Joey, staring insolently across the gurney at Ethan. "Let me see if I've got this straight. You and Joey here believe that the reason he's sick is some radio gizmo that a bug-eyed monster from outer space stuck in his brain. Is that about right?"

"I wouldn't put it that way exactly." Ethan folded his arms across his chest.

Kevin glanced over at Ariel. "Maybe you should run a few tests on *him*. He's as sick as Joey."

"Take a good look at me." Joey clamped his hand over Kevin's wrist.

Kevin drew his eyebrows together and frowned.

"There was some kind of time warp," Joey said. "That's why you grew up and I didn't."

Kevin raised his head slowly to stare at Ethan.

Ethan pushed up his glasses. "It makes a crazy sort of sense, doesn't it?"

Kevin turned his head to appeal to Ariel. "Are you in on this, too?"

Ariel stuffed her hands in the pockets of her lab coat. "I don't know what to believe," she said. "I know that Dr. Kaminsky hasn't been able to find any medical reason why Joey hasn't grown in over two years. It makes Ethan's explanation, however bizarre, less . . . implausible."

Kevin's mouth opened and closed several times, like a fish gulping water. "Okay," he finally managed to say. "Pretend for a minute that I buy all this. Dr. Kaminsky is upstairs in his office right now with Mom and Dad trying to get a call through to some hotshot specialist at UVA. They're talking about flying Joey down to Charlottesville in a helicopter for emergency surgery."

Joey's stomach twisted. They wanted to cut into his brain after all.

"And you think he'd be better off taking a little spin up

to the lake," Kevin said. "Joey is really sick. How is that going to help him?"

Ethan rolled his eyes to the ceiling. "Hanging around all these knife-happy doctors certainly isn't going to."

"What are you talking about?" Kevin demanded.

"Okay," Ethan began. "I think Dr. Kaminsky is right. The object in Joey's head is what's causing his problems. It needs to come out. But ask Ari what Joey's chances are with an operation when there's already massive infection present."

"I don't have to ask her," Kevin said. "I heard what the doctor told my parents. It's not good." He hesitated. "Ten percent maybe."

Joey tried to comprehend what that figure meant. One chance out of ten that he would wake up after surgery. The likelihood of dying was real.

Ariel looked down and squeezed his hand gently with her own. "It is risky," she said. "But Ethan, you just said the transponder, if that's what it is, needs to come out. If not surgically, then how?"

"An alien put it in, an alien should take it out."

A burst of air escaped from Kevin's lips. "Right," he said. "You want to take Joey to meet the . . . the creature that kidnapped him and rammed some thing into his brain. You believe that, and you're still willing to go?"

Ethan didn't reply, his jaw tightening.

"What makes you think it—the alien—would agree to help Joey anyway?" Ariel said.

"What other choice do we have?" Ethan asked.

Joey stared at the panels in the ceiling. The pain in his head had mushroomed, growing so severe that it seemed to have become his entire world. He could no longer remember a time when he hadn't hurt, no longer imagine what it might feel like to stop hurting. Pain was a giant black hole that swallowed up every hope, every memory.

He was beginning to find it difficult to think. Thoughts slipped in and out of his mind before he had a chance to grasp them. He wondered if this was another symptom of the meningitis that was eating his brain. Joey knew he had to speak while he still could.

"The alien might help." Joey's voice sounded weak even to him, but it was loud enough to cause all three heads to turn. "Maybe that's why it's been calling me."

"Yeah, and maybe it's a trap," Kevin said. His voice quivered with suppressed anger.

Joey managed a feeble smile. "See how sick I am? You won't even yell at me."

Kevin didn't smile back.

A strained silence fell over the group.

"Can we have the Jeep, Ari?" Ethan asked.

Ariel glanced down at Joey.

"Please," he said. "It's my best chance."

She nodded almost imperceptibly.

Ethan turned to Kevin. "If you're going to blow the whistle on us, better do it now."

Kevin looked at each of them in turn—Ethan, Ariel, and finally Joey. He squared his shoulders. "Do you honestly think I'd leave you two wackos alone with my brother? I'm coming with you."

"Are you sure this will work?" Kevin asked.

"It won't if we waste time arguing about it," Ariel snapped. "Don't hang around here—get out to the car."

"What about me?" Joey asked.

"You and I are headed to the morgue."

Joey grimaced.

"I'm headed there anyway when the hospital learns I've kidnapped a patient," Ariel said.

"You're not going to get into trouble?" Joey struggled unsuccessfully to raise his head, ignoring the bolts of pain that shot down his neck as he did so.

Ethan enclosed Ariel's hand in his. "I can do this without you."

She shook her head. "You don't have an ID. Somebody might try to stop you." She withdrew her hand and fished her car keys out of the pocket of her lab coat. "So get going."

Ethan accepted the keys, and he and Kevin started down the hall.

Ariel placed the back of her hand against Joey's forehead and frowned. "I just hope I'm doing the right thing."

Joey relaxed a little, calmed by the coolness of Ariel's skin against his hot brow. "You are."

The expression on her face did not change. "Okay, in a second I'm going to pull the blanket over your head. You're dead, remember? I'm sorry about this, but the morgue is off by itself near a back exit from the hospital that no one ever uses. If I tried to carry you out any other way, someone would stop us—you look too sick. Ready?"

In a moment Joey was covered by a blanket. He was unprepared for how unpleasant the soft, smothering weight was against his nose and mouth. He knew that plenty of air could get through the loosely woven fabric of the blanket, but somehow he still felt as if he couldn't breathe.

Pain flared momentarily in Joey's head as Ariel began to push his gurney toward the basement elevator. He heard the ding as the elevator arrived on their floor and the doors slid open. Then his heart stopped as he heard a voice.

"Afternoon, Ariel."

"Good afternoon, Dr. K." Ariel's voice sounded high and tight.

"I hope this is not one of my patients."

"Oh no, this one's not from the ER."

"Since when do lab techs get drafted for the body run?"

It seemed an eternity to Joey before Ariel thought of an answer. "A couple of the orderlies are out with the flu, so we're kind of short-staffed today."

"Really?" Dr. Kaminsky said. "I hadn't heard that."

The elevator dinged again. "Um, well, could you hold the door for me?" Ariel asked. "I don't think it's a good idea if I stand around in the hall too long with this."

Dr. Kaminsky laughed. "No, I guess not."

Joey's heart didn't start pumping again until he felt the elevator start to sink.

Ariel peeled back the blanket from Joey's face. He saw

droplets of sweat glistening in the hairline along her forehead.

"We're almost there, Joey. Let's just hope that no one stopped to chat with Ethan and Kevin."

She pulled the blanket back over his head as the elevator bumped to a halt. Moments later he felt a rush of cold air, then two pairs of arms lifting him off the gurney as Ethan and Kevin carried him to Ariel's waiting car.

CHAPTER EIGHTEEN

Wednesday, October 16, 11:10 A.M.

Joey slipped back and forth across the borders of consciousness, drifting uneasily from reality to delirium. One minute he was balled up in the back seat of the Jeep, his head cradled in Ariel's lap; the next minute he was in the locker room at school. Ms. D'Amato stood there, silver bracelets encasing her arms like chains, demanding that he take a shower in front of the entire gym class. "But I've got an excuse," he told her, as Dr. Kaminsky pulled a sheet up over his face.

The Jeep bounced over a rut in a dirt road deep in the national forest, and Joey was jolted out of one nightmare into another by a detonation of agony in his skull. He gave a small scream.

"Take it easy, Ethan," Ariel said. She stroked the side of Joey's face and tucked the hospital blanket tightly around him.

"Sorry, but this is more like a hiking trail than a road." Ethan stepped on the brake and eased the Jeep to a stop. "I have no clue where we go from here. Any suggestions?"

"Latrine," Joey whispered.

Kevin spoke up from the front passenger seat. "That's where the rangers found his flashlight and sneakers."

"That must be it," Ethan said. "How do I—?"

Kevin didn't let him finish. "Back up. And take the road that loops around the lake. There's a sign that points to a picnic area."

Ethan shifted into reverse, then spun the Jeep forward, stones and dirt shooting out behind the tires.

Joey moaned.

"Be careful!" Ariel snapped.

Almost there. Joey struggled to keep his mind on track, fighting the strange paralysis that crept into his thoughts before he had finished thinking them. He was almost there. He didn't know if he was scared or relieved.

The car bumped to a halt. Ethan switched off the ignition, and there was a rush of cold air as first he and then Kevin stepped out into the graveled parking area adjacent to the picnic grounds.

"We're here," Ariel said. She helped Joey sit up, draping the blanket around his shoulders like a shawl. Kevin reached in and grabbed Joey's arm, and together he and Ariel helped Joey out of the car.

"Is this the place?" Ethan asked.

Joey nodded. The little log latrine stood to his left. Smokewater Lake lay directly in front of him, dark, ringed by somber black trees and the stoop-shouldered mountains beyond. Above it all stretched the silent sky—distant, aloof.

Kevin whistled. "What makes you think anyone from up there would care about us?"

Ethan tilted his head backwards and scanned the sky.

Joey shuddered. Ariel moved closer, wrapping one arm around him. He sagged against her, letting her support the weight that his muscles increasingly were no longer able to bear.

"Ethan," she said in a quiet voice that carried more than a hint of command.

Ethan glanced over at her.

"Are you sure you know what you're doing?"

Ethan stepped closer to Joey. "He's worse, isn't he?" Ethan ran his hands through his hair.

"I'm giving you fifteen minutes. No longer," Ariel said.

Kevin snorted. "So what do we do now, Glass? Hold hands and have a séance? Tell me, genius, just how do you conjure up an alien spaceship?"

"Just wait," Joey said feebly.

And so they waited. The lake was calm, ripples lapping gently against the shore. Dead leaves collected in piles against the legs of the picnic tables, making scratchy noises as they shifted and settled.

Joey remembered the night he was taken, how the earth itself had seemed to breathe, rising and falling beneath the roots of the trees. The lake and even the air had seemed alive, charged with a power that was more than electric. Now everything just seemed dead—dead and still and empty.

There was nothing here.

Suddenly Joey stiffened, the muscles in his body galvanized by a giant spasm. His back arched and he fell to the ground, eyes rolling back in his head.

"What's happening to him?" Kevin asked, his voice rising.

"It's the meningitis, Kevin. Joey's having a convulsion. It should pass soon," she said. "But it's not a good sign."

Joey twitched on the ground, arms and legs jerking, then grew still. His eyes fluttered open.

Ethan crouched down beside Joey. "I steered you wrong, Finney. Ari was right. We shouldn't have come."

"It's kind of late to decide that, isn't it?" Kevin said.

Ethan slid his arms under Joey. "Just give me a hand here, okay, man?"

"Don't," Joey said.

Ethan ignored him. He and Kevin laced their arms together and lifted Joey up.

"Don't worry," Kevin said. "We'll get you back to the hospital before you know it."

"No," Joey repeated.

And then the static flared up again in his ears, roaring through his head like a freight train. It had never been this loud before. Joey clapped his hands to his ears.

"What's wrong?" Ariel asked.

Joey wrinkled his nose. "Smell it?"

Everyone paused and sniffed the air.

"Something's burning," Kevin said.

Ethan looked at Ariel. "It's ozone."

"Ozone?" Kevin said. "What does that mean?"

The headlights of the Jeep started to flash off and on, and they all jumped.

"It's coming," Joey said.

Kevin's eyes widened. "This was a mistake. Let's get out of here now."

Joey felt a tightness in his chest, a tingly feeling. He wasn't sure whether it was fear or excitement. He forced himself to turn his gaze.

"Lake," he said.

Ariel was the first to see it. She gasped; then Ethan and Kevin looked too.

Smokewater Lake was glowing, a milky whiteness from deep beneath the surface silhouetting the papery corpses of leaves floating on the water.

"Put him down," Ethan directed Kevin, and they carefully set Joey on the grass.

Pine needles and fallen leaves started chasing each other in crazy circles along the ground, and there was a feeling like a vacuum, as if the air were being sucked out from around them. Joey felt the same strange looseness in his skin and scalp that he remembered from two years ago. He heard a metallic humming and saw the U.S. FOREST SERVICE sign rotating on its cable until it stood on its head, defying gravity. The earth quaked under their feet.

Ethan stood up. Kevin drew back, barricading himself behind a picnic table. Ariel crouched down beside Joey.

An enormous ball of light rose out of the lake, a swirling mass of color so bright that they all had to squint and shield their eyes.

The vortex opened in the center, like the shutter of a camera lens, and they could see inside it—see through it.

An exact duplicate of Smokewater Lake lay on the other side.

CHAPTER NINETEEN

Kevin's face was distorted with fear. "Where's the space-ship?" he asked.

The silent tornado of light rotated above his head, flashing stripes of many colors across his skin—red, yellow, green, purple, blue.

Joey blinked, trying to see through the glare to the double image of Smokewater Lake. He saw the sky on the other side of the vortex and realized that what he had taken for lights in the dome of a gigantic alien craft must have been thousands of stars. He had never been in a spaceship at all.

"I don't understand," Kevin said. "What's happening?"

For once Ethan was speechless.

"Alice through the looking glass," Ariel whispered.

"What?" Kevin sounded almost angry.

"Don't you see, Kevin?" Ariel said. "It's another Earth, a sort of twin."

Ethan nodded. "A parallel world."

"Door," Joey said. "Lake."

"Yeah, Finney," Ethan agreed. "I think that's what your voice meant. This must be a passage between the two worlds."

A bolt of light streaked down from the vortex and something tumbled down to the shore by the lake. Joey saw a shimmery iridescence, like the rainbows that dance in the spray of a fountain on a sunny day. But this rainbow had a shape, nearly invisible, that gave the impression of a body without one actually being seen.

No one moved. No one spoke.

Joey heard the sound of wind chimes tinkling in his head, the notes forming a melodic pattern that repeated over and over. With a strength he didn't have, he tried to raise himself off the grass to get a clearer look at the shape. It was talking to him, he was sure of it.

Ariel knelt over him. "What's wrong, Joey?"

His lips began to move, but although it was his voice, it was not his thoughts that came out. "The boy is ill. That was not intended."

Joey spoke haltingly, listening to the words inside his head and repeating them aloud a split second later.

Ethan cleared his throat twice before he could say anything. "Was that . . . it? Was that what the alien just told you?"

Joey nodded. He was confused by the voice intruding into his thoughts. It was getting harder and harder to concentrate anyway. He could almost feel neurons dying, whole parts of his brain beginning to shut down. He wondered how much of him was going to be left after this—if there was an after.

Ariel tightened her arms around Joey and glared in the direction of the translucent rainbow-form. "You had no right to take him."

The colors darkened for a moment, and Joey wondered if the alien were ashamed.

"The boy was here. I wanted to keep him."

"He's not a pet," Ariel said.

"I meant no harm."

"That's no excuse," Kevin burst out. "You trapped him like a firefly in a jar. How could you think that wouldn't hurt him?"

"I brought the boy back."

"You left that thing in his head," Ariel said, her voice tight and accusatory.

"I meant no harm," the alien repeated.

"Then take it out," Ethan demanded.

There was silence. Joey lay on the ground, his face ashen.

"That's the only reason we brought him here," Ethan said.

The silence lengthened.

"I can remove it."

Ethan grinned down at Joey. "You're going to be okay, Finney."

Before he had a chance to smile back, Joey heard the voice again in his head.

"I will take him with me now."

"What?" Ethan's grin faded.

"I cannot remove it here."

Joey felt a pang of hope and dread.

"Why not?" Ethan asked.

"It can only be done in my world."

"No way," Kevin said.

Ariel brushed Joey's hair back from his forehead. "Someone help me get him to the car," she said. "We'll take our chances back at the hospital."

The alien's reply sounded flat and unemotional in Joey's head, but Joey's voice trembled when he repeated it. "He will die."

No one said anything.

"Do you not see that he is dying now?"

Cold seeped into Joey's body from the ground beneath him. The alien was right. He had no more time.

Ariel tried to pick Joey up. He fought her weakly.

Kevin stooped down next to Joey "We'll get you back to the hospital. Dr. K will make you well."

Joey shook his head.

"You can't really want to go back with it," Kevin said. "Not after what it did to you before."

Joey's lips started to move. Kevin stooped down and put his ear close so he could hear.

"No choice."

Joey was speaking for himself now.

He looked up into his brother's gray eyes. If Kevin said no, Ethan and Ariel would take him back to the hospital. Somehow he had to convince his brother to let him go. It was his only chance.

"Maybe the alien can cure me," Joey said. "Or maybe it can take me back."

"Take you back?" Kevin said. "Joey, you're not making

sense. What are you talking about?"

"Maybe the alien can take me back before any of this ever happened. Before I got sick. Before you grew up without me."

Kevin glanced over at Ethan and Ariel. "Is that even possible? Have you asked them about it?"

"There's no time." Joey's voice faltered. It took so much energy to speak, more than he could spare as weakness overcame him. "Kevin, please."

Kevin closed his eyes for a moment, then drew upright from Joey and sat very straight. "He wants to do it," he told Ethan and Ariel.

Joey let out a wavering sigh.

Kevin glanced up at the vortex. "I'm going with him."

"No," Ariel said.

"He's my brother." Kevin raised his chin defiantly. "I can't let him go alone."

"Think . . . Mom," Joey said, gulping breath between the words. "Dad."

Kevin lowered his head.

Ethan bent down and hoisted Joey in his arms and began to carry him to the lakeshore where the alien stood.

"When will you bring him back?" Ariel asked.

"In your time?" Joey echoed the alien. "I do not know."

Kevin stepped in front of Ethan and blocked his path. He put his hand on Joey's arm.

"What am I going to tell Mom and Dad?" Kevin asked.

Joey's voice was low but clear. "The truth."

Kevin squeezed Joey's arm, walking alongside him

until Ethan set him down at the edge of the lake.

"It says the door is closing," Joey said. "Leave me."

"I wish I was the one who was going, Finney," Ethan said.

"It's real," Joey said. "You got to see that."

Ethan backed away a few yards and stood his ground, eyes fixed on the light. Kevin, his face grim, turned and ran to the picnic area where Ariel stood.

She reached over and clasped his hand in hers.

"No one will believe us," Kevin said as the vortex began spinning wildly in the sky over the lake.

"Probably not," Ariel said.

"Everyone will think we're crazy."

"It doesn't matter," Ethan said. "We know what we know."

Whirling faster and faster, the colors of the vortex seemed to blend together into a blaze of white. Kevin and Ethan and Ariel saw something like lightning leap between the lake and the sky, and tiny sparks jumped off their skins.

Joey rose through the door to the other Smokewater Lake, and the vortex closed behind him.

The three left behind waited until the ball of light sank back into the lake. When the water faded from white to black, they walked slowly back to the Jeep.

CHAPTER TWENTY

Tuesday, July 5, 1:14 A.M.

He wasn't there, and then he was.

Blackness and silence surrounded him, buoyed him up, so that he felt light and almost bodiless. The vise grip of pain was gone, and even the unrelenting noise in his head was finally quiet.

So this was what it was like to be dead.

Out of habit, Joey sniffed—but there was no fluid, no pus, no blood, nothing to sniff back. His nose was clear. And with the indrawn breath came the sharp, clean odor of pine and the earthy smells of dirt and grass. Grass? Joey opened his eyes. The blackness faded to mere darkness, and Joey heard the gentle sound of water rippling against the shore. The lake. But which version of Smokewater Lake was it? In whose world did it lie—his or the alien's?

He pushed himself off the wet bank and scrambled to his feet, barely stopping to consider the ease and strength with which he could now move. It was night, and the lake was empty and calm. He could see no stars through the lacy canopy of leaves overhead; the sky was obscured by a seamless blanket of clouds. If this was his world, he wondered, why would Kevin and Ariel and Ethan have deserted him here? This was not a good sign. He started to tremble.

Feeling hot, he shed the hospital blanket Ariel had wrapped around him, and stripped off his flannel shirt and sweatshirt. He kept on the turtleneck, but he pushed up the sleeves. Either the weather had grown warmer or he was still running a slight fever. Then he looked up at the trees again, paying attention this time. They were in full leaf.

Joey stood absolutely still for a moment, trying to let his eyes adjust to the darkness, and then he began moving cautiously in the direction where, if this was his world, the latrine and the trail back to the campground should be. After a few yards he stepped on something that rolled under his foot and caused him to crash down to the ground. Muttering harshly, he grabbed the object. It was his old flashlight.

"Dear God," he breathed, his whole body shaking. "Please."

Joey switched on the flashlight, and seeing a pair of castoff sneakers, began to run up the trail. He leapt over his old shoes, unimportant now except for the scary rush of hope they gave him. What if he was wrong? Panting, he reached the edge of the woods and swung the beam of the flashlight around a large clearing. His knees almost gave way beneath him.

There was the pup tent where his mother and father were sleeping the night he disappeared, and there was the boxy old canvas tent.

Joey walked toward the larger tent slowly, uncertainly.

He pushed back the flap and shone the flashlight inside. Magnum raised his head sleepily, then caught a whiff of Joey and began to probe him in earnest with a wet nose. Joey wrapped his arms around the dog and gazed at the sleeping bags lying on the tent floor, one of them unzipped as if someone had just left it.

He turned his light on one bag and saw with satisfaction the pudgy face of the old Hamp. He turned his light on another and saw Kevin, looking like a little brother again. Joey sighed. He was going to miss the Kevin who had, in a different future, offered to go with him through the door in the lake. He thought about his sister Molly and realized with a pang that she hadn't yet been born. Maybe coming back wasn't the answer he thought it would be. Who could he talk to about everything that had happened to him? Who would believe the truth?

Joey tilted his head back and stared for a long time at the blank slate of the sky. Finally he nodded to himself and went inside the tent. He stepped over Hamp, then leaned down and put his hand on his brother's shoulder.

"Kevin," he whispered, bending over and cupping his hand to his brother's ear. "I've got something to tell you."

Nancy Butts is also the author of a novel for older readers, *Cheshire Moon* (Front Street). She lives in Barnesville, Georgia, with her husband, their son, and three dogs.